F.E.A.R

FACE EVERYTHING AND RECOVER

YOUR SANITY

F.E.A.R. YOUR SANITY

Acknowledgements

Thank you, Almighty God, for bringing me through every valley and allowing me to see that I was never there alone.

Thank you to the horizon to my sky, my lovely spouse, soulmate and best friend, Kimberly. Kim, you are the shoelaces to my sneakers. Thank you for your support. Through all seasons, I vow to love you and choose you today, tomorrow and always.

This book is dedicated to my one and only son, Makai. Son, you are my sunshine and the personification of love. You have helped me to become a better version of myself. You are an inspiration and I love you more than words could ever express. Thank you for being my greatest joy and for changing my life. Being your mom is a blessing and I could not be prouder. My love for you is immense and I hope that it shows through my nurturing, actions of appreciation, love, devotion, guidance, regard, and respect.

This book was not easy to write but I did it. May its completion be an example to you to never give up on your dreams. Never grow weary or tire from working to achieve your goals. Pursue your goals and dreams with the intent of making them a reality. Always persevere through the ups and downs that will surely come as they are a part of life. Lastly, always stay true to who you are. I love you forever and always.

F.E.A.R. YOUR SANITY

Panic

Approaching my third anniversary in Washington, D.C, I could not be more pleased with my decision to leave my hometown of East Orange, a middle-class neighborhood of northern New Jersey. As a successful political novelist, I had already gained national notoriety for seven of the ten popular political thrillers I had written that landed me in the top rankings on the New York best-sellers fiction list. While it is always an ongoing goal of mine to continue to dwell on the best-sellers list, I had even bigger dreams that extended outside of the scope of the literature world. I dreamed of entering political media and journalism.

As a child, my stepdad taught me about the importance of social equity, civic engagement, and how it all relates to politics. Ever since then I have been hooked. I achieved a Bachelor of Arts degree in Sociology and a Master of Political Science degree. Nearly twenty years later and I am nationally recognized as one of the best political writers of all time.

After having appeared as a guest commentator for various shows at MSNBC television cable network, I was presented with an offer that I simply could not resist. I gladly accepted a permanent spot as a political analyst on a popular national news platform, Joy Reid's The ReidOut, one of MSNBC's top political conversation shows. Joy Reid was not only one of the best correspondents in the business, she also was a dear friend and mentor.

I was hired with the intent to help the network reach a more diverse audience and I certainly was up for the task. In my role, I work alongside the star, Joy Reid, and with a few other analysts. Collectively, the vibrant spectrum of The ReidOut offers a political voice to the often marginalized black and brown demographic. The journey traveled proves that dreams do come true, even if they take a while to come to fruition. This indeed was a dream after having gone through a lot of changes in my personal life including a bitter breakdown and complete separation from the majority of my immediate family. So, when the opportunity presented itself, I gladly uprooted my husband, Warren, and our son Kyle from New Jersey and transplanted south of Washington D.C. in the upscale neighborhood of Old Town Alexandria, an affluent section of Alexandria, Virginia.

After work, I grabbed a few groceries at Whole Foods and headed home. My husband, Warren is a practicing attorney and law professor at Howard University's School of Law. He works long hours and per the usual would not be home until after eight o'clock. Similarly, our son Kyle is a senior in high school and will be at basketball practice until after 7 o'clock. With it only being noon, I had plenty of time to relax a bit before getting dinner started.

F.E.A.R. YOUR SANITY

To the same extent as accepting the perfect job, the home that we purchased three years ago is a true depiction of life's possibilities when you work hard and in a field that you love. Built six years earlier in 2015, our home is beautiful and situated on a quiet cul-de-sac with only seven other homes on the block. With it being mid-October, the autumn foliage is breathtaking every time I pull up to the gated entrance of the exclusive community. Our home backs the scenic views of Strawberry Run Stream Restoration and Fort Taylor Park, a historical landmark with over 90 acres of natural imagery. Inside of our colonial-style home are six bedrooms, five bathrooms, high nine-foot ceilings, and exclusive details that includes crown molding, wainscoting, and custom wood window shutters. The main level is completely all white with a light-filled open floor concept that includes formal living and dining rooms with incredibly huge bay windows to the gourmet kitchen with a center island and marble countertops. The second floor is just as beautiful with built-in bookshelves in the study, a large main suite with an impressive stone fireplace sitting area, two matching his and her walk-in closets, and a large main bathroom with a soaking tub. The level of delight and gratitude that I have is immense. Never in a million years could I ever have imagined this level of achievement coming from where I am from. God's promises for my life exceeded my expectations and for that, I have so much to be thankful for.

Glad to finally be home, I prepared a bath, lit some Lalique candles from the Voyage de Parfumeur collection, and undressed into my Fleur du Mal angel sleeved silk mauve-colored robe. I sashayed over to the wet bar within our main suite to prepare a glass of champagne. It was an impromptu celebration of a wonderful three years in the D.C. area. I sipped on Korbel as I submerged all of me into the warm bath in the oversized standalone bathtub. Sonja Marie's And I Gave My Love to You filled my bathroom oasis when I suddenly heard a noise. Quickly silencing the music, I listened intently for the noise again. There it was, this time it was more repetitive tapping followed by a pinging sound. In an instant, my body went from a zen state of mind to complete panic-stricken. My eyes widened as fear took over me. I jumped out of the bathtub, grabbed my cell phone, and bolted into one of the walk-in closets. I hid under my neatly organized wardrobe and nervously dialed for help.

"Hello, 911, what is your emergency?" the woman said on the other end of the phone.

"I have an emergency, someone is in my house, send help," I spoke in a low speaking voice trying to keep my voice down.

"Ma'am try to remain calm. Explain to me what is happening. Who is in your house?" she asked.

Panting uncontrollably and consumed with fear, I tried to slow my breathing, "I am home alone. I live in Rafton

Estates, and someone is here in my house. I can hear them," I huffed.

"I am sending a unit to your address ma'am. Do you live at 555 Fortress Park Lane?" asked the woman.

"Yes, please hurry, I am in danger," I quickly hung up so that I could listen for more noises. Thankfully, there were none. In less than five minutes I could hear the police sirens approaching. Feeling somewhat relieved, but still afraid to come out of the closet, I stayed put. A few minutes later my cell phone rang, and I quickly answered so that the potential intruders could not trace my location.

"Hello, this is Officer Floyd, are you Ms. Rasheedah Taylor? I am here at your address with the security guards, from the front gate. Ma'am can you please open up?" the officer asked.

"How do I know you are a police officer?" my voice shook as I tried to catch my breath.

"Uh, because I am dressed in uniform and my squad car is out front. Please open up the door and speak with me," he spoke with concern.

"Okay, I will come downstairs. Can you please stay on the line?" I asked as I quickly dressed and sprinted downstairs to the front door. I opened the door relieved to see the police and two of the security officers responsible for permitting vehicles in and out of the wrought iron security gate that safeguarded the entire Rafton Estates community. There is a staff of over twenty full-time security guards working around the clock 24-hours a day, 365-days a year. Yet, I felt unsafe.

"Oh my God, thank you so much! I was upstairs enjoying a bath when suddenly I heard some loud thumping noises. I had no idea who or what was inside," I exclaimed as the officers and guards stared at me strangely. I was a mess and visibly shaken. My hair was all over the place and it was evident that I had been crying. The officer tried to reassure me that everything was okay.

"Ms. Taylor we'd be happy to survey the grounds outside as well as inside to ensure that no one is in your home. But do you see these big guys right here?" the officer pointed at the security guards, "these armed gentlemen are hired to protect all of the residents here and so I am confident that this is all just one big misunderstanding," he said.

I began to cry, "yes, please check because I heard the noises several times."

"Of course. Let's check things out, guys," the police officer said leading the guards into the foyer. They checked inside the property as well as on the outside. All clear.

Another security guard arrived, as the officer and other guards were exiting my home, holding a large floral arrangement. "Apologies for the hassle, Ms. Taylor. You had a floral arrangement that was delivered a few minutes ago. When residents are not home to accept deliveries, they are left at the guardhouse. What you might have heard was the driver ringing your doorbell or knocking loudly on the door. So sorry that he startled you," he said with a regretful look on his face. The arrangement was from MSNBC and the card read, 'Happy 3rd Anniversary, we could not be happier with you being a part of the team'.

I was embarrassed. Uneasy and completely humiliated, I shut the large oak door, and quickly locked myself in. I climbed the flight of steps and returned to my bedroom feeling like an idiot. I cried inconsolably for hours. Finally fed up with living life in panic, I grabbed my phone and googled therapists near Alexandria, Virginia. I called the first name that showed up, Isaiah Franklin.

April 1983

"Hey, Sandra! Sandra, buzz me in," a man yelled from outside.

Shaken and afraid, Sandra ignored the man calling for her from the sidewalk. She refused to go to the window and was adamant that she would not buzz the man in. She was convinced that doing so would only cause more problems. "Please leave," she silently thought to herself as she slowly walked into the bathroom to clean her face. At five months pregnant, Sandra looked more like eight months pregnant but still a lovely sight to see. Her full jet black naturally curly hair, high cheekbones, perfectly arched brows and 5-foot-8-inch statuette frame was still slender except for her round protruding belly. Sandra was 'all belly' according to family and friends and did not exhibit any of the typical physical signs of pregnancy like most women. She was naturally beautiful and glowed even more while pregnant.

Sandra was in the bathroom at the sink cleaning herself up. She applied a cold washcloth and flinched as her face stung from the red-stained cloth. Her face was tender to the touch as she nursed a bloodied nose and busted swollen lip.

Then there was a loud boom. The noise startled her so much that she dropped the damp washcloth and hurriedly shut the bathroom door. Closing herself in, she squatted down behind the bathroom door and softly pleaded, "please God, please God".

"Sandra, open the door," the man yelled.

Apparently, the man had made it into the apartment building after all and was now yelling for Sandra to open the door from the hallway. She never did buzz him in but suspected that the man must have entered following behind one of her neighbors who had keys to the main door downstairs. Now he was on the fourth floor standing at her door frantically banging for her to let him in. Sandra was hiding in the bathroom behind the door when her live-in boyfriend began shouting.

"Who the fuck is it?" yelled the man from inside of the apartment. "Sandra, get your ass out here," the man angrily shouted. "Who did you call over here?" he asked.

Terrified, Sandra emerged from the bathroom holding her belly as she slowly walked over to the front door, joining her boyfriend, Keith, in the living room of her one-bedroom apartment.

"I did not call anyone over here," she replied to Keith.

"Sandra, let me in!" the man kept shouting from the hallway.

"Richard, I'll talk to you later, go on home. I am alright," she spoke calmly to the man on the other side of the door. Her intention was to appear normal and to not cause any alarm to her 19-year-old brother.

"Sandra, open this door before I kick this shit in! Enough is enough," Richard yelled. Sandra could hear that there were additional male voices in the hallway demanding that she "open up the door," but she still refused.

"Richard, no don't do that," Sandra exclaimed as her brother and his friends began kicking the door. After three kicks, the men kicked the door in. The door flew ajar, and all of the men rushed into the apartment.

Richard and four other men stormed inside of the apartment and attacked Keith. Unable to fend the men off, Keith staggered through the living room attempting to getaway. There was nowhere to escape. They lived in a small one-bedroom apartment on a fourth-floor walkup. In tandem, the men took turns punching and kicking Keith, condemning him between each blow, for beating on Sandra, his pregnant girlfriend.

"Don't you ever, in your muthafucking life put your muthafucking hands on my sister again," Richard said through gritted teeth while stomping Keith in the head. "Fight a man, muthafucker! Try doing that shit to a fucking man," he exclaimed angrily.

Sandra paced back and forth with tears rolling down her face. One of the men, a tall stocky man with a dark complexion walked over and hugged her. "Sis, you don't deserve this. Why didn't you call me the first time that coward put his hands on you? Richard is like a little brother to me which means you are my sister. Family looks out for family," he said releasing her from his embrace and looking into her eyes. His eyes enlarged

12

and grew with rage when he noticed her busted swollen lip and a bloody nose.

"I don't know why he keeps doing this," Sandra sobbed. "He gets so drunk and gets out of control, Peanut."

Enraged with fury, Peanut ran over to join the others in beating Keith beyond recognition. The furniture toppled over as one of the men yelled, "let's throw his bitch ass out the window!" The others smiled in agreement.

Satisfied with the suggestion, Peanut picked Keith up by his collar and the others helped to carry him towards the open window.

"Don't kill me, man! Don't kill me! That bitch is lying, man," Keith pleaded for mercy.

"Who the fuck are you calling a bitch?! You are the bitch-ass coward for hitting a pregnant woman! You deserve to die, muthafucker!" Peanut yelled. Peanut held his grip while the others held up each of Keith's legs. Keith was squirming and screaming for help as the men held him dangling outside of the window. Onlookers four stories down watched in shock, as the men yelled profanities at Keith before releasing him into the air. As he was thrown from the window Sandra screamed in horror, "oh my God!". She rushed to the window and watched Keith's body hit the pavement. Witnesses stood over him asking if he was okay. He lay still with his eyes tightly shut.

Sandra could overhear a passerby shout, "they fucked his ass up for hitting that woman again, huh". Another woman laughed, "that is what your punk ass gets for hurting a pregnant woman. She is too pretty for your ugly ass anyway," she taunted while standing over Keith.

"You do not like the way it feels to get hit by men, do you? Hope this teaches your drunk ass a lesson to stop beating on her," another woman spat at the beaten man lying limp on the pavement before walking away.

"What have you done, what have you done," Sandra cried looking at the five men as Richard shut the window and pulled the shade down as if it were a normal April afternoon. He turned to face his sister.

"Sandra, I cannot believe you have sympathy for a muthafucker that did that to your face! Look at yourself! He stomped you out like a man in the fucking street! How dare you care about him, are you crazy?" Richard yelled at his older sister. "Had Chantel not heard him whooping your ass, and called me at the house, I never would have known," Richard continued.

"Yeah, thank God Chantel called you little bro. Word is bond, I wish I had known sooner what that clown ass drunk was up to over here," Peanut said shaking his head. "Y'all help me straighten up this mess," Peanut said referring to the disheveled living room. He and the other men begin cleaning up the disarrayed living room. Sandra stood in silence as she watched the men pick up the overturned furniture and sweep up the remnants of the shattered lamps and vases, she had bought from Kmart months earlier.

As the men reorganized the living room, the sound of an ambulance siren grew louder. Then the sound of police sirens followed.

The men were unphased by the noise and continued to clean. Richard, the youngest of the bunch, walked over to the window and peeped outside from behind the shade. He saw two paramedics providing medical aid to an unconscious bloodied Keith and the police asking onlookers for information about what had happened. "Oh shit, 5-0 outside asking people what happened," Richard said as he began to panic.

Peanut calmly replied with confidence, "ain't nobody gonna rat, trust me. That sorry ass got what was coming to him. Now, go check on your sister, she went into the bathroom." Richard followed Peanut's directive. He met his sister in the bathroom where she had gone to wash her face, again.

"You're gonna be okay, Sandy. That clown-ass coward deserved what he got," Richard said as he touched his sister's shoulder. "You should go stay with Piggy for the night just until you calm down. You don't need that muthafucker, me and Piggy are your family, that drunk loser ain't your family," he declared referring to himself and his other older sister.

"You are right, Richard," Sandra said as she turned to face her brother.

15

"Go pack a bag. We'll walk with you over to Piggy's," he said.

"Wait, I have to get Scooby ready, he's in the bedroom," she said.

"Oh shit, Scooby was here the whole time when he was beating on you? Richard asked as he exited the bathroom and rushed towards the bedroom. As they walked out of the bathroom, they met Peanut in the living room holding a teary-eyed shaken three-year-old shirtless toddler. Rodney, affectionately known as Scooby due to his love of the cartoon, Scooby-Doo Where Are You, was crying for his mother when Sandra appeared. "Here I am Scooby, your mommy is here," she held her arms out to receive her son, whose diaper was sagging and soaking wet.

"Mommy, I hate Keith," the little boy whined.

Sandra looked at her son and shook her head, "mommy is here. I am so sorry he scared you. Let's go to see your aunt Piggy," she said embracing Scooby tightly.

The April sunshine was still beaming when the group left Sandra's apartment altogether. Sandra lived on 18th Avenue in the city of Newark, diagonally across from West Side Park. Despite the violent incident that occurred an hour prior, the block resumed buzzing. Cars were passing through, neighbors were sitting in chairs chatting together out front of the apartment buildings, patrons were entering and exiting the corner bodega which was feet away from Sandra's doorstep. Things seemingly had gone back to normal.

Scooby was in better spirits as he sat in his stroller playing with his wrestling action figures.

"Hey, Scooby! How are you," asked an older woman sitting out front of Sandra's building.

Scooby gave a warm smile as he cheerfully greeted the woman, "hi there."

"Hi, Ms. Rose," Sandra spoke to the woman.

"Hey, Sandra. Hello, gentlemen," her neighbor greeted Sandra and the others.

"Hello," they all said in unison.

No one uttered a word about the incident.

Peanut and the others departed exchanging high-fives and hugs with Richard, Sandra, and Scooby before they began walking down 18th Avenue towards Springfield Avenue. Sandra pushed Scooby in the stroller the opposite way of 18th Avenue as Richard accompanied her to Piggy's apartment located on South 17th Street about a mile away.

Piggy was sitting out front on her stoop talking with neighbors when they arrived.

"Piggy!!" Scooby cheerfully greeted his aunt.

"Hey there, my boy! Come give your aunt some sugar," Piggy affectionately greeted her nephew. She picked Scooby up from the stroller to give him a hug and kiss as he giggled with expectation.

"Alright, y'all I'll be on Springfield with the guys. Sandy, you and Scooby need to stay here for the night," he stated as he walked away to go join his friends.

"Sandy, why did Rich have to walk you... Wait, what the hell happened to your face?" she yelled as she noticed Sandra's swollen lip.

Piggy's neighbors tried getting a good look at Sandra, but Piggy was now standing directly in front of her sister, intentionally blocking their view.

Although Sandra was the oldest of the three siblings, she was timid and also had the reputation of being the prissy pretty girl. Born and raised in the rough streets of Newark, New Jersey, Sandra would fight if and when she had to but was far less confrontational than both Piggy and Richard, who were her younger siblings. Piggy was only a year younger than Sandra, but at 20-years-old, she was twice Sandra's size. Debra is her real name but family and friends affectionately nicknamed her Piggy due to her stout frame. Out of the three of them, Piggy had a reputation of being a fighter who hardly ever backed down.

"I'll speak with y'all later," Piggy said as she motioned for Sandra to come inside of the apartment. Sandra rushed inside as Debra lifted Scooby and his stroller up the 8-step stoop.

"Ok, talk with you later Piggy," they said as she slammed the front door that led to her apartment.

Upon arriving in Piggy's apartment Sandra asked, "Where is Andre?" as she walked towards the couch.

"At his grandma's place. Now, Sandra, I know damn well that ugly muthafucker did not put his hands on you, again. When will you get tired enough to leave his black ass alone?" Piggy asked.

"Piggy, this time I am tired. I cannot take it no more," Sandra defeatedly replied.

"Yeah, Sandy just stop with the dumb shit! I have heard you say that same shit more than once before. He has been wailing on your ass from the start. At what point is enough, enough? And now you go and have a baby for his sorry ass. Now, you are stuck," said Piggy as she lit up a cigarette and took a hard pull.

"It is not like I wanted his fucking baby, Piggy. I don't even like fucking his short dick ass. Keith never can even last five minutes," Sandra exclaimed shaking her head.

"Wait! You a goddamn lie, bitch you told me he was a good lay," Piggy responded with a hearty laugh. "So, let me get this straight, Sandy. He's whooping on your ass and he cannot fuck? You're a silly bitch to keep putting up with his bullshit," Debra exclaimed.

"No! What I told you was I only gave him the time of day because he had a nice car. That's what got his ugly ass the time of day but then when I got to know him I found out he eat coochie really good," Sandra said matter-of-factly as she reached into Scooby's diaper bag for her cigarettes.

"Bitch, he be too damn drunk! Can he even find the pussy?" Piggy joked.

"Hell-muthafucking-no, and that's a problem," Sandra replied. The women fell out laughing.

Sandra lit a cigarette and took a pull and then a deep breath. Smoking while pregnant was nothing new for her. She had smoked cigarettes during her entire pregnancy with Rodney, therefore her current pregnancy was no exception. Smoking while pregnant was not taboo during the 1970s and 1980s. In fact, it was typical for pregnant women to indulge in smoking cigarettes as well as indulging in small intakes of alcohol.

"Keith drinks too much for me and every time he gets drunk, he wants to beat on my ass. I am tired of it, and I am tired of him. I only got with him to make Brooks jealous," Sandra admitted referring to her ex-boyfriend and Scooby's father, Brooks. "Richard and his friends whooped his ass girl and threw him out the window. Scared me half to death," said Sandra.

"I wish I was there to help them do it! I would've used a baseball bat to beat that son of a bitch's teeth out his mouth! So, are y'all finally over now? You are pregnant with his baby which means he will always be in the picture," Piggy said sounding disappointed.

"Not for long," Sandra said.

"What do you mean?" Piggy replied expecting further explanation.

"Just like I said, not for long," Sandra said not wanting to give further explanation.

"Bitch, explain yourself," Piggy shouted with frustration. Her annoyed projection startled Scooby, who was walking around his aunt's living room exploring how to use the television remote control.

"I cannot have this baby, Piggy. I am going to the clinic to get rid of it. If I don't, I will be forced to deal with Keith and his crazy-ass mother for the rest of my life. I am done with his ugly ass for good this time," Sandra confessed.

"Well technically, you would only be stuck with him until the baby is grown, so until it turns eighteen. Girl, can you imagine if that baby comes out looking just like his black ugly ass? Oh dear Lord, return to sender," Piggy laughed.

"Ain't no need in imagining shit. I am not keeping it, Piggy," said Sandra.

"Sandy, I think you too far along to get rid of that baby. Why the fuck would you wait so long if you didn't want to keep it? How far along are you, about five or six months?" Piggy asked.

"I will be nineteen weeks next Monday. It is not too late because Jamilah did the same thing and she was five months or better," said Sandra referring to a friend of hers.

"Oh okay, well do that shit because your life would be better off without him in it," Piggy said.

"Yeah, I'm going to call them tomorrow. I need to make an appointment right away," she said, satisfied that her sister approved of her decision to abort the baby.

"Will Medicaid pay for abortions that far along?" Piggy questioned.

"I don't know, I hope they will. All of my other abortions were under three months, so I don't know. I will find out tomorrow," replied Sandra.

"Did you cook anything? I am starving like Marvin," Sandra asked changing the subject.

"I damn sure didn't, I got a taste for some fried porgies though," Piggy said.

"Well, I can buy the fish, if you are willing to fry it. I got plenty of food stamps. I never went shopping because Keith drunk ass was too drunk to take me to the supermarket," she said reaching for Scooby's diaper bag to retrieve her wallet.

"Dammit, I left my goddamn stamps on the dresser in my room. I hope his ass didn't steal my shit before he got his ass whooped!" Sandra jumped up in a frantic panic.

"I doubt it, but let's walk over there to get the stamps. I will walk to the fish market. You and Scooby can come back here to my place and relax. Andre's grandmother will be dropping him off later tonight," Piggy said.

They exited Piggy's apartment and headed back to Sandra's place. In the distance, as they approached the apartment building, they saw two women standing out front. One of the women seemed to be yelling at the other, although Sandra and Piggy could not hear the full nature of the conversation.

As they walked closer, they could hear and see very clearly who was out front.

"She ain't nothing but a piece of trash! I told my son, from day one, not to involve himself with that welfare recipient. She ain't got shit, and never will have shit! Got some nerve getting those sorry ass thugs to beat on and throw my son out of a fucking window," the woman yelled at the other woman who stood shaking her head in agreement.

"I understand you are hurt, Miss Cynthia. Wow, I can just feel it," Miss Rose spoke with dramatic sympathy as she listened to Keith's mother, who was dressed for confrontation in a grey sweatsuit and white Reebok sneakers.

"They could have killed my baby! Do you realize that?" Miss Cynthia continued venting to Miss Rose, not noticing Sandra, Piggy, and Scooby approaching the apartment. Miss Rose noticed the three and immediately put on a smile and cheerfully spoke, "hey, Scooby, there goes my boy again. How are you, little man?" Miss Rose asked as Scooby smiled and waved his hands.

"What the fuck are you doing at my sister's house? Your sorry excuse of a son ain't here! So, what the fuck do you want?" Piggy asked as she stood in Miss Cynthia's face shouting.

"Who the fuck are you talking to? I am here to speak to this bitch for telling them boys to hurt my baby! You need to step aside and mind your own goddamn business, Piggy!" yelled Cynthia fumbling around in her purse as if she were looking for something. She never took her eyes off of Piggy.

"I didn't tell nobody to do anything, Miss Taylor," Sandra said referring to Keith's mom by her last name. Despite what was going on between her and Keith, she still tried to respect his mother.

"Sandra, take Scooby upstairs! I need to give this old bitch a piece of my muthafucking mind!" Debra faced Miss Cynthia with rage in her eyes.

"Your baby is a 23-year-old boy who likes to get pissy drunk and punch on my sister like she's a fucking man! Your baby is a bitch ass woman beater for hitting on my sister while she is five months pregnant with his fucking baby! He got his ass whooped today! And keep fucking with me, you next in line!" shouted Piggy stepping closer to Miss Cynthia. While Piggy was an aggressive 20-year-old with a proven record to fight grown men twice her size, Miss Cynthia was no easy contender. She too had a reputation to be ruthless and was only

24

36-years-old since she had Keith at the age of 13-years old in the backwoods of Chesterfield, South Carolina.

"Piggy stop! She ain't worth it. I am done with her son. Let's go inside," Sandra said.

"No, this fat sloppy bitch said she can whoop my ass. I would like to see her try," Miss Cynthia said withdrawing a blade from her purse that she had finally located. "I will slice your ass up like a piece of ham, bitch! You have tested the wrong one today," Cynthia exclaimed waving the blade.

Piggy pushed Sandra out of the way as she pulled out a boxcutter from her back pocket, "bitch, please, when I'm done with your old ass, you will need an ambulance, just like your ugly ass son did earlier." The ladies squared up preparing for a faceoff, both of them swinging blades as Sandra, Miss Rose and passersby looked on.

Piggy approached Cynthia preparing to take a slice of her neck when Scooby began to scream, "no, no, no! No aunt Piggy, you better not hurt my Penny!" Scooby said referring to Cynthia, the only grandmother he'd ever known since she came into his life two years earlier. Scooby nicknamed Cynthia, Penny, because she was the first to put pennies into his piggy bank. The two often spent lots of time together. Penny was Scooby's caregiver when Sandra and Keith were on good terms and went out to spend time together.

It was the loud cries of a child that ended the fight between the women. Cynthia looked at Scooby with a face of brokenness, "Scooby, never forget that your Penny loves you. I have taken care of you when your own sorry ass mama had no food to eat or no place to sleep before her section 8 kicked in. I will always love you and think of you, Scooby. Remember that," Cynthia kissed his hand and turned away to leave.

"Penny, come back," Scooby cried, extending his arms reaching for his grandmother but Cynthia kept walking.

"Sandra, you made your bed, now you got to lay in it. I am sending Keith back to South Carolina, you will never see my son ever again, bitch. He doesn't need you and he doesn't need this! You are a piece of trash and were never worth his time," Cynthia walked off.

"Now I see why Keith ain't shit, it's because his mother ain't shit either! Piggy shouted at Miss Cynthia who was nearing the corner of the block.

"The apple does not fall too far from the muthafucking tree! Listen to her Sandra. She is sending that sorry excuse of a man away. She is ok with him running away from his responsibilities. What kind of grandmother doesn't even care about their own flesh and fucking blood," said Piggy referring to the unborn baby that she'd just given approval for Sandra to abort moments prior.

Cynthia stopped and turned around, "that baby ain't his! Why do you think Keith came over here to beat her ass! I told him everything that I saw! He knows your slutty sister was hugged up with Brooks in Westside Park while Keith was at work. She ain't nothing but a skank whore," Cynthia shouted back.

"You and your son can go to hell! I never wanted his black, ugly little dick ass anyway! Fuck you, bitch," yelled Sandra as Cynthia turned the corner and was finally out of sight.

"Sandy, you need to make that appointment ASAP!" Piggy advised.

"I damn sure do, quick, fast, and in a hurry! I will call Monday morning" Sandra replied.

Sandra and Piggy took Scooby inside.

*

Two days later, Sandra awoke to a hungry three-year-old. Scooby was jumping up and down on the bed, "Mommy, wake up! I am hungry," he exclaimed.

"Boy, sit your ass down and stop jumping on this bed!" Sandra hollered.

Scooby stopped at once, "ok, mommy, I am sorry," he said as he climbed off the bed and ran into the living room.

Scooby immediately recognized that his mom was in a bad mood. He was used to his mother yelling at him out of frustration of issues that had nothing to do with him. Most times, when his mother seemed mad or frustrated, Scooby would go play in the living room with his favorite action figures, WWF wrestling men. He mostly enjoyed WWF because of the legend wrestler, Hulk Hogan. So, whenever his mom was upset and needed space, Scooby entertained himself by playing with his toys or watching television.

Sandra's mood worsened as she recalled the events that had taken place days ago on Friday. She was met with mixed emotions. Relief was the first emotion as she was glad that the beatings were finally over. The days of Keith staggering into the apartment drunk were over. As were him punching and slapping her until he was out of breath and she was balled up in a fetal position. No more forcing her to have sex with him until he passed out.

The second emotion was sadness. She was upset that she had to learn from Miss Cynthia that Keith was leaving New Jersey and moving back to his birthplace of South Carolina. While she was the first to openly admit that Keith was not what she found physically appealing in a man, she was disappointed that he had up and left without trying to fight for their relationship. She sat at the kitchen table confused and upset, angrily wondering to herself 'how the fuck could he just leave me without saying goodbye knowing damn well I'm pregnant with his first child.' She was angry as she unsuccessfully fought back tears.

As her thoughts took over, Sandra began to sob. The more she thought about what had occurred, the more she regretted joining Brooks in the park one afternoon when he had come to visit Scooby. Sandra knew that she and Brooks were over. He had made that clear after informing her that his current girlfriend was pregnant again with their second child. Scooby already had a sister and now a baby brother was on the way. Despite these circumstances, Sandra was still in love with him and never rejected Brooks's sexual advances towards her. So, the thought that Miss Cynthia told Keith about what she had witnessed sickened her. Sandra knew that things were over for good with Keith. She mentally convinced herself that she could not afford a second baby and had to immediately terminate the pregnancy. She was unemployed, and was already struggling financially to provide for Scooby. There was no room for a second baby.

Sandra lit a cigarette as she dialed up a place that she had grown familiar with over the years.

"Good morning, thank you for calling Planned Parenthood. This is Helen speaking. How may I help you?" the woman asked on the other end.

"Yes, I'm calling to make an appointment," Sandra said as she walked into the living room to check on Scooby before returning back to sit at the kitchen table. Scooby was sitting on the sofa watching television and playing with his Hulk Hogan and Andre the Giant wrestling toys.

"What type of service is this appointment for?" the woman asked.

"An abortion," Sandra replied.

"How far along are you in the pregnancy ma'am?" Helen asked.

"About fifteen weeks," Sandra lied. She was fully aware that she was nearing the twenty-week mark. She feared that Helen would have never booked her an appointment had she'd been truthful of how advanced she was in the pregnancy.

"We have availability for Thursday, April 14th. I will need some additional details to confirm your appointment. Please provide me your full name, date of birth, and type of insurance," Helen said.

Sandra provided her with the requested information and ended the call. She boiled some Arnold's sausages and then scrambled some eggs.

"Scooby, come eat. Breakfast is ready," she said. Scooby hurried into the kitchen with a huge smile on his face, "thank you, mommy. My tummy is making loud sounds" he growled imitating his stomach.

*

Thursday arrived faster than usual. All week long, Sandra tried reaching Keith to confirm whether or not he had gone back to South Carolina, but he was unreachable. Every time she called Miss Cynthia's house, Keith, who would usually answer the phone almost always, never did. When someone did pick up, it was always Miss Cynthia, during which Sandra would quickly hang up the phone.

In recent arguments, the most he would stay away from Sandra would be a day or two, three days at most. This time, Keith was nowhere to be found. While she did not doubt that he left, she did not want to take his mother's word without confirming it for herself. Pondering at her reality that she was once again left alone to raise a baby on her own without any paternal help, created a sense of emptiness. Sandra had gone through similar circumstances three years prior with Scooby's father, Brooks. She had never come to terms with accepting his abandonment of she and their son, but now she was preparing to experience the same thing with Keith.

She lit up a cigarette and dialed her sister's phone number.

"Hello?" Piggy answered on the first ring.

"Hey, it's me. Can you watch Scooby while I go and get this shit over and done with?" Sandra spoke with frustration.

"Yeah, you want me and Andre to come there, or are you gonna drop him off over here?" Piggy asked.

"You know what, if you don't mind, can you come over here? I may not have the strength to come pick him up afterwards when I am done," Sandra said as her lips quivered.

"Okay, I can do that. I will leave my house in the next 10-15 minutes," Piggy replied. She could hear the disappointment in Sandra's voice. It hurt Piggy to bear witness to her older sister going through yet another heartbreak and yet another abortion. It was all becoming too routine.

Sandra was an attractive caramel complexion woman who got a lot of attention from men. They found her attractive and often pursued her until she finally gave in to them. While she enjoyed their pursuits, she never could sustain a long-term relationship with any of them. Once their needs were met, each of the men would either leave her completely for someone else or meet someone new and keep Sandra on the backburner. Although she enjoyed the attention, Sandra wanted to be with someone who would never leave. She'd suffered from major abandonment issues since the age of 8-years-old.

Once the call ended, Piggy and her two-year-old son, Andre, left and headed over to Sandra's house.

F.E.A.R. YOUR SANITY

You Will Just Have To Keep This One

The taxicab pulled up to the front of the grey stone building where a large crowd of people gathered. The crowd of twelve to fifteen men and women stood with signs of all shapes and colors, chanting "pro-life, pro-life! I say pro, you say life! Pro-life, pro-life!"

As Sandra exited the taxicab, one of the protestors grabbed her by the arm and another exclaimed, "murderer!! Babies have rights, who are you to end a human life," a male protestor screamed in Sandra's face.

"Get your muthafucking hands off of me," Sandra shouted as she snatched her arm away from the stranger. As Sandra walked towards the entrance of Planned Parenthood, she joined a smaller group of women who were also headed for the entrance. As they hurried towards the building, the women were ambushed by the crowd of protestors. They ran towards the women and continued shouting pro-life chants and calling them "murderers!" One of the protestors ran ahead of the women and laid on the ground in front of the building. Other protestors followed her lead and created a human chain in an attempt to block the entrance to the clinic.

Staff members of Planned Parenthood forced the doors open, knocking a few of the protestors to the ground, and pulling in the women one at a time until all seven of them were safely indoors.

"Hurry in ladies, have a seat. Someone will be with you shortly," said one of the staffers in a low voice as she tried to catch her breath.

One by one each of the women was called into the back. As Sandra patiently awaited her turn, she felt relieved to see that she was not the only woman in the waiting room visibly pregnant. She and two other women's bellies were protruding and of the three of them, Sandra's belly was the smallest.

"How far along are you," asked the woman who seemed further along than all of the women.

Damn, how did she know that I was thinking that same thing, Sandra wondered to herself how far along the other ladies were.

"I'm four months," Sandra said looking directly at the woman, hoping she would volunteer how far along she was in gestation.

"I am five fucking months and I have no fucking shame! I already got four bad ass kids and cannot afford a fifth one," the woman confessed without shame.

"I understand," all of the remaining women replied in unison.

Then the room grew silent.

"Sandra Peterson?" a nurse holding a clipboard called for her. Sandra stood up and headed to the back as the doors closed and locked behind her.

"How are you today, Ms. Peterson?" the woman asked as Sandra walked behind her.

"I'm ok," Sandra replied.

"We're going into room 4 to do an ultrasound. I will take your insurance information and ask you a few additional questions at that time," she said.

"Ok," Sandra replied.

They arrived in the room and Sandra provided a copy of her Medicaid card to the woman.

"Okay, please undress from the bottom down and then lay on the table," the woman instructed.

Sandra did as she was told. The woman placed a generous amount of warm jelly onto Sandra's belly and navigated the probe across her growing bump.

"How far along did you say you were, again, Ms. Peterson?" the woman asked as she looked at the screen that illustrated an active moving object.

"I don't know exactly. I think I am close to four months," Sandra lied.

The woman looked at Sandra and replied, "try six months."

Sandra was stunned. While she was aware that she had surpassed four months she was baffled to learn that she was much further along than twenty weeks.

"Our organization cannot administer terminations past eighteen weeks of gestation. You, my dear, are twenty-five weeks pregnant. It is too late to abort this baby girl," she said matter-of-factly as she wiped away the jelly off of Sandra's belly.

A baby girl? Sandra was stunned. "I cannot believe I am that far along," Sandra sat up from the examination table with tears filling the rim of her eyes.

"Yes, you are approaching the seventh-month mark. We can offer you prenatal care, but you are certainly beyond the abortion timeframe. You will just have to have this one. Get dress and meet me out front," the woman spoke in a nonchalant tone before exiting the room.

*

Sandra arrived back at her apartment uncertain. The news that she'd received at the clinic left her with more questions than answers, and with more frustration than confidence.

She slowly walked up the steps wondering how was she going to fair raising two children alone. Things had already been difficult raising Rodney with little to no help from Brooks. How would she do this? Her lip began to quiver and the tears began to fall again. There was no way she would be able to manage two kids with no job and no support from their daddies.

Sandra was halfway up the steps when she turned to face the more than thirty steps she'd just climbed. She closed her eyes and jumped. She grunted as she violently tumbled down the steps and landed on her back. Piggy, along with Sandra's neighbors each opened their doors to see where the noise was coming from.

"Sandra, wholly shit!!!" Piggy ran down the steps to run to her sister's aide.

"Oh my god, Sandy! Are you alright??! How the fuck did you fall down the steps?" Piggy asked frightened about her sister's condition.

"Piggy, you want me to call the ambulance?" asked one of the neighbors.

"Yeah, call 911!!" she yelled but was interjected by a visibly hurt Sandra.

"No! I'm alright, don't call no ambulance," Sandra responded, trying to pick herself up.

Piggy helped Sandra up the stairs and they walked slowly into the apartment. Sandra sat at the kitchen table in silence.

"Sandy, what the fuck happened? Are you feeling weak from the abortion?" Piggy asked with concern.

"I did not get one," Sandra replied.

"What?" Piggy looked confused.

"I did not get an abortion, Piggy. Them bastards told me I am too far along. They said I am close to seven months fucking pregnant!" Sandra yelled.

"Oh shit, I would've never thought you'd be that far along, Sandy," Piggy replied.

"I don't know what the fuck I'm gonna do with two fucking kids," Sandra said, as she began to cry again.

Piggy walked over to her sister and hugged her. Sandra sobbed without cease, "I don't know how I'm gonna take care of two fucking kids," she cried.

Piggy rubbed her big sister's back repeatedly as she reassured her, "I'll help out as best as I can, Sandy. We have always managed to figure shit out as it comes our way. Me and Richard will do whatever we got to do to help. Don't worry, everything will be alright. We all we got. Just, watch you will see. Everything will be okay."

"I hope so, Piggy," Sandra said.

My name is Rasheedah-Keitha Taylor

"Rasheedah?" "Rasheedah! Rasheedah, are you okay? Should we take a break?" my therapist asked as I quickly opened my eyes, startled by him projecting his voice. I could not hear Isaiah calling my name until he shouted "Rasheedah" the second time, that is when I opened my eyes. I was resting uncomfortably on Isaiah's cognac brown leather couch when he snapped me out of this episode of oversharing.

"Sorry to interrupt the story. I only interrupted you because you are trembling," he spoke as he handed me a Kleenex to wipe away tears that I had not realized were falling from my eyes.

"Isaiah, I am alright," I said rising up from the sofa. "It is just difficult to talk about. I often think to myself, 'damn, she really tried to get rid of me.' It certainly explains a lot but that is alright," I continued.

"Rasheedah, no, that is not alright and no, you are not alright. The first step in the healing process is allowing yourself to be honest with what you are feeling. Stop trying to convince yourself of this false notion that you are okay when it is apparent that you are not okay. Over the years you have tried to condition yourself to believe that you are alright. However, the truth is, you have experienced significant trauma from early on," he spoke affirmatively. "As a result of the traumatic events you have experienced, you live a life of fear. In fact, you seem to be paralyzed by fear. My goal is to try to identify ways to help you cope with trauma," he looked at me.

I looked away from Isaiah attempting to avoid eye contact. For as long as I can remember I have always felt uncomfortable when anyone looks at me for too long.

"Well, she tried but she failed! Despite several attempts to self-terminate the pregnancy, I prematurely made my debut into the world," I loudly proclaimed shifting my train of thought. "There were significant complications during the delivery that almost hindered me from gracing the world with my presence. Mother had hemorrhaged from inserting a hanger into her vagina. That is what brought on the preterm labor. She was rushed to the hospital, and I was delivered via c-section at thirty-two weeks. She did not want me, but I am still here, I made it," I laughed awkwardly.

"My mother named me, Rasheedah-Keitha Taylor after my father, Keith Taylor. What a name, right? I have no middle name, Rasheedah-Keitha is one name. Keitha is not a middle name, Rasheedah-Keitha sounds like a run-on sentence. As much as Mother despised Keith, she gave me his name, which I thought odd. That is until I was old enough to ask her why she named me after someone she hated."

"Because you came out looking exactly just like that black muthafucker! I mean damn it was just so unbelievable Rasheedah. I was praying to God that you would look like me but nope. I wanted you to have my hair, skin tone and body shape. Nope! You came out looking just like his black ass. Talk about pissed off. You were and still is Keith's mirrored image. You look nothing like me at all," Mother said to me at the age of seven-years-old. I know for a fact that I was seven-years-old because I was in the first grade at the time.

The following day at school during roll call the teacher began calling each student's name. When she asked, "Rasheedah-Keitha Taylor are you present?" I recall yelling at the teacher, "that is not my name, don't ever call me that again. My name is Rasheedah Taylor," I said correcting my teacher. "Mrs. Lecheko had looked at me like I'd lost my damn mind. I must have looked crazy attacking that woman for calling me by my name. From that moment onward no one ever called me by my full name, I was Rasheedah Taylor going forward," I said.

"Wow, and is it because you did not like having two first names or because of the correlation to your father?" Isaiah asked.

"It is because Mother always referred to my father as black and ugly, and so for her to say I looked just like him made me feel that I, too was black and ugly. She would always make comments about my dark skin and beady eyes and how I was Keith's clone," I sadly said. "Isaiah, I try to block a lot out, honestly. The more I try to forget about the past, the more certain experiences resurface. I decided on counseling because the past seems to come up more and more often here lately.

"Now that I am here in counseling, I hate to talk about the past. It causes me to be overwhelmingly emotional. Crying is so exhausting. I just have a hard time speaking about my life," I said.

"How has sweeping things under the carpet worked for you over the years?" Isaiah asked.

"It has not served me well at all," I shrugged.

"Well from what you have just shared, I have a few questions. The first question is, how do you know about the specifics of what occurred that led to your father leaving the state? Secondly, and just as important to that question, who informed you of your mother allegedly seeking to abort you?" he asked with a blank stare.

"My mother and aunt told me," I replied matter-of-factly.

Isaiah sat up in his chair. With his glasses resting on the edge of his round nose, Isaiah looked surprised.

"Now wait for a second, Rasheedah. So, your mother and aunt went into detail about all of this? Even the part about your mom throwing herself down the stairs?" he asked.

"Yes," I flatly responded as the tears welled up in my eyes, "she never wanted me from day one, which is why I was treated like a piece of shit growing up," I replied.

"I am very sorry to hear that, Rasheedah. I must say that it does explain a lot about the strained relationship between you and your mother right now in the present. Okay, let's wrap it up for today. Given that today was so heavy, I will await our next session to offer you some clinical feedback," Isaiah said.

"Okay," I said feeling relieved that the session was over.

I left Isaiah's office and made my way to the parking lot. With only a few sessions under my belt, I pondered not attending another appointment. Without failure, each therapy session had left me exhausted and somber. I had only been going for a few months and had considered suspending therapy after each meeting. I did not like opening up and felt that therapy was causing more harm far more than it was helping. While I did feel that it has somewhat helped me to identify what created my issues of panicking and not being able to sleep at night, my woes of battling anxiety still existed. They have been part of my life for as long as I could remember and I still had not figured out how to resolve or even cope. The decision to pursue therapy again came about because the anxiety has gotten worse. I was hoping that therapy would offer an immediate result that would put a stop to my anxiety altogether.

It was after 7pm when I walked out of Isaiah's office feeling unsettled. I looked around to see if any strangers were lurking. Once the coast was clear, I sprinted to my car, quickly hopped in, and locked the doors. Once the doors were locked, I felt safe from the outside. Panting and trying to catch my breath I sat still for a few seconds thanking God that I had made it to my car safely. As I put on my seatbelt I stopped in my tracks.

"What a damn shame. Grown as hell, nearly forty-years-old and still afraid of being outside at night," I spoke aloud shaking my head with disappointment. "Or in the daylight for that matter," I shook my head annoyed with my conduct.

Isaiah was right, I am paralyzed with fear and cannot even recall a time that I was not afraid. Afraid of no particular person or thing. I am fearful to go into unknown places, or dark places or of people staring at me, or of what others think of me. Living with anxiety has often angered me and today was no exception.

"Man, I fucking hate this," I yelled as I hit the steering wheel.

The more I thought about my life, the angrier I grew. Here I am, an adult in the physical sense but a scared child mentally more often than not. In my mind, fear and anxiety are signs of weakness. Yet, I have struggled with feeling weak and powerless my entire life. I hate the idea of appearing weak in any regard.

Counseling has only magnified my feeling weak and scared like a child. It was clear, I needed to end my therapy as it has only made matters worse. This evening was my final therapy session, and that's that, I declared to myself.

I held the brake pedal and started the engine to my brand new 2021 matte black Mercedes G-Wagon with deep cranberry red leather interior but then I stopped in my tracks. Instead of driving off, I dialed Isaiah's phone number.

"Hello, Isaiah. Rasheedah Taylor here," I announced myself.

"Yes, I know. Hello, Rasheedah," he replied.

"I would like to cancel all future appointments. This is just too much to handle," I announced.

"When will you give yourself permission to live free from the bondage of your past?" Isaiah asked.

"Isaiah, I have been sitting in my car outside in the parking lot for quite some time thinking about this whole therapy thing. I really cannot commit to therapy right now. The truth is, since starting therapy I have been an emotional wreck. My anxiety has not improved but has worsened. I am still not sleeping and in addition to not sleeping, I find myself abruptly crying. I only cry when I think about the past, but the thing is, speaking about the past makes me think about it even more. I have an image to uphold and a successful career to maintain. I have a family. Despite my anguish, my life does not stop. I have to be present for my family and for my business endeavors," I blurted without any breaths in between.

"Okay. I see," Isaiah continued to listen.

"Yes, and I feel that speaking about all of the horrors of my life makes me even more irate with those who are close to me. I have been hell to live with over the past couple of weeks and my husband Warren and son, Kyle, are bearing the brunt of my mood swings. I need to take a break," I said concluding my argument.

"Rasheedah, I am just wrapping up notes for tonight's session. Quite frankly, you exhibit symptoms of someone suffering with post-traumatic stress disorder. I suspect that much of your fear and anxiety stems from being the victim of multiple sexual assaults and emotional abuse endured from your childhood and adolescence. Of course, I understand that speaking of your past is not easy. It will continue to be difficult to speak of the trauma you have suffered. Yet, the healing comes from opening up. Therefore, I would encourage you not to withdraw prematurely before getting help on how to heal from some very traumatic events. Again, yes, it surely is understandable why you would prefer to evade discussions about hurtful experiences that have caused you a great deal of pain. I can reassure you that by committing to seeking help, as time goes on you will find that these sessions offer you relief as will the treatment plan. The purpose is to provide solutions to cope with trauma.

Retracing the steps of a painful past is certain to be troubling. It requires an individual to dig deep into the rawest and vulnerable of places. My goal as your therapist is to create an environment that is a safe space to speak freely about whatever you are comfortable with sharing. And we certainly, can proceed slowly at your pace. It is, however, important that you understand that you are a survivor of substantial chronic trauma that dates back over thirty years. So, when you look at it from that lens, it will take time to heal. Recovery is gradual and will not happen overnight. I encourage you to be patient with yourself and the process" Isaiah said.

I remained silent and continued to listen.

"I understand that you are a private person with a family of your own. The goal is not to upset you or have you emotional at every appointment. Emotions are typically high at the start of a therapeutic journey. But you cannot run from your experiences. The truth is this, your trauma already manifests in many ways that you may or may not be aware of. The experiences from your past are impacting your personal as well as professional life in some way, shape, or form. It will take time to identify the indications and of course with the most appropriate treatment plan, therapy can help identify potential resolutions on how to triumph over tragic circumstances" Isaiah continued.

"Rasheedah, are you there?" he asked.

"Yes, yes I am. I hear you, Isaiah," I replied.

"Okay great. So, please give it some time. You have my word that we will proceed at your pace. And if you find that my structure does not suit you, feel free to create a structure that you are most comfortable with. Going forward we can proceed with whatever topic or occurrences you are comfortable with" he assured.

"Okay, Isaiah. Sounds like you are not accepting me running away," I laughed.

"Not one bit! It is far too early. Please do not throw in the towel. You owe it to yourself," he said.

"Okay, I am fine to proceed as long as we can do so in a way that I am comfortable," I said.

"Of course, Rasheedah. You have my word," Isaiah said.

"Ok great. Guess I won't be canceling my standing appointments after all. I would like to speak about some specific occurrences from the past that I believe contribute to my ongoing feeling fearful and in panic mode" I said.

"Okay, and I will offer clinical feedback at the end. Sounds good?" he asked.

"Yes, sounds good. Thank you," I replied.

TRAUMA* trau·ma | \ ˈtrȯ-mə also ˈtrau̇- \

1 a: an injury (such as a wound) to living tissue caused by an extrinsic agent

  b: a disordered psychic or behavioral state resulting from severe mental or

    emotional stress or physical injury

  c: an emotional upset the personal trauma of an executive who is not

    living up to his own expectations

2   an agent, force, or mechanism that causes trauma

*As defined by Merriam-Webster. (n.d.). Citation. In Merriam-Webster.com dictionary. Retrieved January 15, 2021, from https://www.merriam-webster.com/dictionary/citation

Meet Me Where I Am

I arrived a half-hour early to the next session. I walked into the office building with my purple suede journal in tow confident that I had made the right decision to continue with therapy. I had finally come to a place where I no longer wanted to allow my anxiety to control my life. It took years but I finally acknowledged that I needed help to heal from a fucked up childhood.

Typically, I am guarded when it comes to matters of the heart. When I am troubled I either hold everything in and overanalyze the issue in my head repeatedly. Other times I confide in Lorraine, my best friend of over thirty years. Lorraine and I have been through thick and thin and she is more like a sister than a friend to me. If I ever needed someone to listen, or a shoulder to cry on I could always rely on Lorraine to offer that support. However, there are some things that I have not even felt comfortable sharing with Lorraine as it concerns my past. I just have kept those matters close to my chest and chose not to share them with a soul. In fact, I have tried to wipe a lot from my own memory hoping that the memories would fade away.

Counseling would be no exception. I would only reveal what I felt comfortable discussing full stop, I thought to myself as I entered into Isaiah's office.

F.E.A.R. YOUR SANITY

"How is it going, Rasheedah? You are early today," Isaiah interrupted my thoughts as I sat in the waiting room.

"Hello, Isaiah. Yes, I was scheduled off of work today, so I figured I'd leave home a little early to beat the traffic. Hope that you don't mind," I said with a smile.

"Of course, that is no problem. I will be right with you," he replied as he headed towards the restroom.

I am pleased that Isaiah agreed to help me heal on my terms. For years I avoided seeing a therapist because of negative experiences. Connection is very important to me. Previously I had two failed experiences with therapists who I felt did not understand me. In my mind, if a therapist cannot relate to me then surely it would be impossible to create an environment that will foster my healing from anything.

So far, the journey with Isaiah was completely the opposite of what I had experienced before with the other therapists. Isaiah is a black psychotherapist who is a little older than me. He and his wife Reena had been married since they were twenty-years-old and had six children. I do not think it was Isaiah's background or age that made the difference in our connection. He was different from the other therapists because I felt comfortable expressing my raw truth without feeling judged. While he may not relate to my life, he made me feel like my experiences were not taboo or unrelatable. I also appreciated that he allowed me to receive therapy at a pace and structure I was comfortable with.

"So, where would you like to start?" he asked.

"Umm," I froze. "I don't know. What topic should I cover, where should I begin?" I asked.

"This is your session and as we have agreed, we will go where you want to go at a pace you are comfortable with. So, you let me know where you feel comfortable starting" he replied.

"There is so much. I honestly do not know where to start," I admitted.

"And that is okay, Rasheedah. Let's do this, if I asked you to give me four words that sum up your life experiences dating back as far as you can remember until today, what would those words be? Isaiah asked.

I sat still for a moment to reflect on my life. It surely has been a journey filled with pain, disappointment, some happiness and hurt.

"I'd say trauma, destruction, perseverance, and restoration," I said.

"Very good. The first word that came to your mind was trauma so that is where you should begin. Before you do, let's define what exactly trauma is. For the sake of discussion, I will define the two common types of trauma by sharing the clinical definitions.

The first type is known as acute trauma. Acute trauma stems from "a single distressing event, such as an accident, rape, assault, or natural disaster. The event is extreme enough to threaten the person's emotional or physical security. The event creates a lasting impression on the person's mind. If not addressed through medical help, it can affect the way the person thinks and behaves. Acute trauma generally presents in the form of excessive anxiety or panic, irritation, confusion, inability to have a restful sleep, feeling of disconnection from the surroundings, unreasonable lack of trust, inability to focus on work or studies, lack of self-care or grooming; aggressive behavior," (Allarakha, 2018, p.1).

The second type is known as chronic trauma. Chronic Trauma deals with the long term as opposed to incremental or short term and "it happens when a person is exposed to multiple, long-term, and/or prolonged distressing, traumatic events over an extended period. Chronic trauma may result from a long-term serious illness, sexual abuse, domestic violence, bullying, and exposure to extreme situations, such as a war. Several events of acute trauma, as well as untreated acute trauma, may progress into chronic trauma. The symptoms of chronic trauma often appear after a long time, even years after the event. The symptoms are deeply distressing and may manifest as labile or unpredictable emotional outbursts, anxiety, extreme anger, flashbacks, fatigue, body aches, headaches, and nausea. These individuals may have trust issues, and hence, they do not have stable relationships or jobs. Help from a qualified psychologist is necessary to make the person recover from the distressing symptoms," (Allarakha, 2018, p.1).

Now that we have established what trauma is, speak to me about the trauma you have experienced in your life," Isaiah said.

"Okay here goes nothing," I said as I slowly opened the beautiful purple book and began to speak the dark and ugly truth.

My Protector, My Hero, My Friend

"Little Jimmy is coming y'all! Little Jimmy," all of the neighborhood kids exclaimed. They could see the local Italian ice truck slowly making its way down the block from afar.

It was a hot June afternoon and I, along with Rodney and Rahmel, were visiting Rahmel's grandfather's house. We always liked going over there because their block was packed with kids our age with whom we attended school. We normally walked there after school while our mother worked her part-time evening job.

Rahmel's father, Miles, was our mother's first husband. Rodney and I had different fathers but Mother was never married to either of them. Though Mother was legally married to Miles, she and Miles lived in separate households and maintained separate lives. Domestic violence and infidelity played a major role in their separation.

Despite their separation, Mother still maintained a relationship with Miles's family that consisted of dozens of extended uncles, aunts, and cousins. During the week, Miles's father, Samuel, who was a Vietnam vet as well as the undeclared neighborhood lieutenant of the block, sometimes allowed us to come over and play with the other kids until one of us did something he didn't like. Then he'd run us off his block by cussing and fussing. Most times, Samuel was mean to us. He only tolerated us because of his love for Miles.

"Daddy, it's Little Jimmy! Can I have a dollar?" asked Mile's youngest son, Jabriel, who was being raised by his grandfather Samuel rather than his father, Miles.

"Go upstairs and look under my ashtray," he answered.

Excited and patiently waiting for the arrival of the Italian ice truck, all of the kids had their dollars in their hands waiting for Little Jimmy. It was the highlight of everyone's day.

Jabriel ran upstairs as fast as he could and retrieved the money that Samuel had under the ashtray. Like clockwork, Little Jimmy arrived right in front of Samuel's house where all of the neighborhood kids stood patiently. Samuel gave Jabriel a dollar and he went to join the other kids waiting in line. Me, Rodney, and Rahmel looked at Samuel with pleading eyes hoping he'd be just as generous to us.

"Samuel, can we please have a dollar, too?" I spoke for myself and my brothers.

"Goddammit, hell fucking no! I ain't got money to give every goddamn kid in the neighborhood money for ice cream. Your mother should have given y'all money! In fact, call her to come to get y'all muthafucking begging asses," he screamed.

He was shouting so loud as if making a public announcement for the entire neighborhood to hear was his intention. All of the kids laughed as we walked away with nothing from the Little Jimmy truck. I ran into the house embarrassed and ashamed as Rodney and Rahmel stayed outside and continued to look on at the other kids. Mile's older cousin, Shirleen, laughed even harder than the kids, intentionally to upset Rodney.

"Look at her ugly ass running in the house mad over some damn ice cream," she cackled obnoxiously as Samuel joined in.

"Their goddamn mother should have given them money. It's not my problem," Samuel said throwing his hands up in the air.

"Why does my sister got to be called ugly? You a grown woman making fun of a little kid. You must feel really good about yourself doing something like that to a child," Rodney angrily yelled at Shirleen.

"Boy shut the fuck up! I can say whatever the fuck I want," Shirleen exclaimed.

"Okay. If my sister is ugly so is your fat, crusty-mouthed daughter," Rodney exclaimed referring to Shirleen's daughter, Shante.

"Sam, you better get him before I fuck him up," Shirleen threatened.

"Yeah whatever, I'd like to see you try," Rodney replied refusing to back down. He got upset and announced that he was taking us home. "Rahmel, we are leaving! Go get Rasheedah so that we can go," Rodney spoke with authority.

"Nobody gives a fuck about y'all little bastards leaving," Shirleen declared as Samuel shook his head in agreement.

"You goddamn right. I know I sure don't give a fuck," Samuel said.

"Rahmel, go now!" Rodney said ignoring all further comments from Shirleen and Samuel.

"Ok, Rodney, I will go get her," Rahmel sadly replied with tears in his eyes. He slowly walked towards Samuel's house but got sidetracked as he stopped and stared at the other children eating their Italian ices.

I was too humiliated to go back outside with the other kids so I sat on the couch in Samuel's living room praying that our mom would hurry here to come to pick us up.

I sat for less than five minutes when one of Samuel's three sons, Timothy, came into the living room demanding that I go back outside.

"Take your black ugly ass back outside, I'm watching Video Soul," he said.

"I just wanted to watch TV until my mother comes to get us," I replied sadly.

"Why are you in here, while all of the other kids are playing outside? What, they don't want to be bothered with your big-teethed ass? Too black and too ugly?" he said coldly.

"No," I held back tears until I no longer could. "All the other kids are eating ice cream and we don't have none," I said.

"Who are we?" he asked.

"Me and my brothers. We asked Samuel but he said no to us," I whined.

"Haha Haha!" That's what your ugly ass gets!" Timothy taunted and laughed aloud.

Timothy was an eighteen-year-old cruel jerk especially towards me and my oldest brother Rodney. Given that we technically were not related to any of them, it was Rahmel who was related to them, Samuel or his three sons were never nice to Rodney or me.

I sat silently staring at the television but was not paying attention to Video Soul at all. All that I could hear replaying in my mind were the harsh words that Timothy had spoken. Not realizing that tears were falling from my eyes, I blankly stared at the screen and wished for me and my brothers to be home with our own ice cream watching our own television and playing together.

Timothy sat and stared at the television for a couple of minutes before he realized that I was crying. Rather than having sympathy for hurting my feelings, he taunted more.

"Now you are already ugly as hell, you making yourself look even worse by crying, blackie!" he laughed. "That is why all of the girls laugh at you because you are black as shoe polish with big rabbit teeth and nappy hair," he laughed even harder.

"The only thing you got going for yourself are those big nice tits but even they don't make you look no better because you are still an ugly buck teeth bitch," he exclaimed.

I was so hurt that my heart felt like it was too heavy to remain in my chest. I cried so much and so hard that it turned into sobs and it was hard to catch my breath. I jumped up and ran from the living room into the bathroom where I could cry to myself without having someone laugh.

When I got into the bathroom, I looked in the mirror and cried even harder when I looked at the reflection staring back at me. Maybe, I was ugly and black as midnight. It was true that my teeth and chest were the only things that poked out. I cried because everything that Timothy, his brothers, and all of the other kids at school said were right, I was a black, buck-teethed, nappy-headed bitch that nobody liked.

I was wiping my face when Timothy opened the door to the bathroom and walked in, closing and locking the door behind him. He stared at me with disgust on his face as snot and tears continued to roll down my face. My eyes were bloodshot red and my face looked ashy from over-wiping my face with toilet tissue.

He looked at me and shook his head with disgust in his eyes, "wipe your nose!" he ordered.

I wiped my nose with no outcome because snot and tears continued to run down my face.

"Come here!" he ordered again as he unzipped his jeans. A strong musty odor filled the narrow bathroom as Timothy dropped his pants to the floor revealing his teenage body.

I obliged his orders by slowly walking over to him afraid that he would call me more names. He reached into his boxer briefs and pulled out his erect penis demanding that I touch him, "grab it. Wrap both hands around it. I will give you some cream from my dick," he scoffed. Timothy's voice had changed from loud and authoritative to a low and anxious voice as he stared at me with a mischievous smirk.

He guided my hands forcing me to stroke his penis as he grabbed and squeezed my breasts. My breasts were unusually large for my age. I was overdeveloped and was the only kid with C-cup breasts. I had always hated having large breasts because I was made fun of and taunted by the boys yet hated by other girls my age. At this moment, I really hated my breasts. Timothy's touch was harsh and his eyes filled with anger as I told him my breasts hurt. Each time he squeezed them hard I screamed, "ouch, Timothy they hurt!" I cried.

"Shut the fuck up! Go up and down on my dick bitch, oh yeah! Keep going, keep going!" he grunted.

"Harder, harder, more... tighter," he said breathing heavily.

I followed his orders until he moaned loudly, releasing warm semen all over my hands. "Eww, what is that?" I asked completely grossed out. At only eight years old, I was confused by what had just happened.

"It's milk. You said you wanted some ice cream," he laughed sarcastically.

He grabbed some toilet paper and wiped himself free of what he described as "milk". When he was finished, he looked at me and said, "damn that shit felt so good! And you better not say one-word blackie," then he exited the bathroom.

I washed my hands off, wiped the remaining tears off of my face, and then left the bathroom. It seemed like I'd been in there for hours, but Timothy's enjoyment had taken less than ten minutes.

I walked out of Samuel's house and was headed towards the steps when I saw Rahmel walking towards the front door.

"Rodney said that we have to go," Rahmel said.

"Good, I hate it here," I began to cry again confused and afraid at what had just happened.

"What's wrong, Rasheedah?" Rahmel asked. "Are you sad because you didn't get any ice cream?

"No! I don't want any ice cream," I cried even harder thinking about what Timothy said and did.

Rodney hurried over to join Rahmel and me on the steps of Samuel's house.

"Rasheedah, where were you?" Rodney yelled at me.

"I was in the bathroom, Rodney," I mumbled, trying to stop the tears as they continued to well up in my eyelids from falling.

"Rasheedah, what is wrong? Tell me right now. Why are you crying?" he stared at me with fire and concern in his eyes.

I stood and looked at my older brother ashamed. The tears kept flowing as I cried nonstop. I cried because I afraid to tell my brothers what Timothy did but I also was extremely uncomfortable due to my sore breasts. Presently shaken and confused I replied, "nothing's wrong Rodney," I said as the tears rolled down my face and my heart raced a mile a minute.

Rahmel looked on as Rodney grew angry and concerned for me. "Rasheedah, what happened?" He walked closer and put his arm on my shoulder to comfort me. He lifted my bowed head up and looked into my eyes, "did someone do something or say something wrong to you in there? Tell me right now, who hurt you?" Rodney asked.

"No one, Rodney," I lied. "I'm just sad that I am black and ugly, that is all," I said.

The tears would not stop.

Rodney leaned down and hugged me tightly, "Rasheedah you are not ugly! Do not ever say that again! Do you hear me? And black is not a bad thing, black is beautiful. We are all black so fuck these people and what they think.

Come on y'all, we are going home. We out of here," he said grabbing my hand and leading me and my younger brother Rahmel away from Samuel's house.

Relieved that we were going home, I smiled and squeezed each of my brothers' hands. Rodney led us eight blocks to the doorsteps of our two-bedroom flat. Arriving home was so welcoming. We sat in our own living room watching our own television while eating our own food. It was such a safe space and relief after what I had gone through earlier. For the rest of the evening, I forced myself to forget about what Timothy had physically done. Although the physical attack was painful, his words were far more difficult to block out of my mind.

Our mother never showed up that night, so Rodney made us a pot of ramen noodles for dinner and put us to bed. He was such a great brother to Rahmel and me. At only twelve-years-old, Rodney served as a surrogate paternal figure, and we respected him as such. He was tasked with having to take care of his two younger siblings and did everything he could to ensure that we were okay. I was so thankful for him that day and so many other days ahead.

I owe a lot to Rodney for not only being a great big brother but for being my protector, hero, and friend. He shielded Rahmel and me as best as he could from the things that he was aware of and for that I will be forever grateful.

Something In My Heart

Rahmel's father, Miles, was in and out of our lives. While he and Mother had been married for several years, their relationship was off and on. Sometimes they would take breaks in the relationship. Their breakups were unsolicited by our mother and mostly initiated by Miles. Mother loved Miles more than anything in the world, including her own children. When Miles was around Mother was around. She would come straight home after work, she would cook for us, we would watch movies together as a family, or even go places together. When things were good between Mother and Miles, my brothers and I were hardly ever left home alone. Mother was a different person when Miles was around. Whatever Miles asked of Mother she obliged without hesitation. She did everything to please Miles but for some reason, their moments of marital bliss were always short-lived. The two would constantly argue and as time went on the arguments had turned physical. The altercations turned into brutal sometimes bloody drag-outs and my brothers and I witnessed the evolution.

The truth is Miles had created a whole other family while married to Mother with his girlfriend, Yvette. He had met Yvette while working as a janitor at East Orange General Hospital. Yvette was a nurse there. As things progressed between the two of them, Miles began staying overnight some evenings with Yvette across town. He even became an active role in Yvette's daughter, Kristin's life and she eventually started calling him "daddy". Kristin and I both were the same age, but she looked completely different from me. She was light skin, skinny, and pretty. She did not have breasts at all and was a normal-looking eight-year-old.

Given his new relationship, Miles was back and forth between being present in our lives, living with us in our apartment with Mother, demanding that Rodney and I call him "daddy", just as Rahmel and Kristin did, to not being around at all. His time out of the house progressed. It went from sparingly to once or twice a week to never being home at all. And when he was home, he would only be there long enough to start a fight with Mother so that he could leave to be with Yvette. Mother would often scream "you are leaving your family to go be with that bitch! Fuck you muthafucker!" Then there were times when Miles would swoon Mother into believing he desired to save the marriage.

"I love you, Sandra. I finally told Yvette it is over, and that I am working things out with my wife," he would often lie. His lies became so routine that I recall memorizing his lines. Yet, Mother would always have faith in the lies he told her. It was a vicious cycle that would happen constantly. Miles would leave for a while, and we would not see nor hear from him. Then he would come back begging and pleading, telling Mother the same lies. She would accept him back into her life and into the home, only for him to repeat the same cycle.

A few months had gone by, and Miles and Mother were doing well. He was not staying out overnight, and neither was she. Everything seemed great until one day Mother shattered our world.

"Kids get dressed so that we can go get something to eat," Mother said.

"Where are we going, Mommy?" I asked with excitement as my brothers hurried to put on their socks and shoes.

"Girl you always got to be in the know. You always have questions, just go get ready," Mother replied.

"Mommy, can you take the three of us to McDonald's?" I asked while putting on my shoes. Between my brothers and me, I always spoke up on behalf of the three of us when I was not afraid.

"Yes, Rasheedah, that is where I was taking y'all, mouth almighty," she shook her head as she put on her coat.

"Yay, I am riding shotgun!" I called it before either of my brothers could.

We got into Mother's minivan and she turned on the radio and lit up a cigarette. She quickly took in two deep pulls. Grey smoke filled the air of the minivan, so I rolled the window down.

"Leave the damn window alone, Rasheedah! Rodney, make sure Rahmel is fastened in," Mother said, in between puffs, referring to our youngest brother who was only four years old.

"He is, Mommy," Rodney replied.

We drove a few blocks before I began turning the knob to find a good song on the radio. Music was a great escape for me. Music and reading books to be exact. At home I would read books or watch music videos on The Box or on BET, using my hairbrush to sing along with the different artists. On the way to McDonald's, there was a new R&B artist singing over the airwaves, Michel'le. Michel'le was lighting up the charts with her unique sound. I reached for the radio knob to turn up the volume because she was singing one of my favorite songs, Something in My Heart.

"Oh, I love this song! She sounds so different from the other singers and she is so pretty!" I spoke with excitement as I began to sing along. "When I grow up, I want to be pretty just like Michel'le. I want to wear nice clothes. I want to get my hair done and wear it long down my back. I want to wear pretty lipstick and get my nails done just like her," I continued to harmonize in tandem with Michel'le.

"Rasheedah, turn that shit down! I need to talk to y'all and here you go acting like you ain't got no sense," Mother yelled. I turned the radio off completely.

"Bitch, I said to turn it down, not off! Try to listen to what you are being told sometimes, Rasheedah," she shouted, and I quickly turned the radio back on and turned the volume down very low, which I did not get the point of having the radio on at all since I could no longer hear anything. Michel'le was now whispering about the changes she was going through and how her life is forever changed and never would be the same.

"Your daddy and I have been talking about this for a while now. We have decided the best way to make more money for the family is to go into the army. I am leaving," Mother slowly spoke as we waited for our turn at the drive-through at the McDonald's. I hate when she referred to Miles as "our daddy", he was no daddy of mine or Rodney's, he was Rahmel's daddy. We all had different fathers. Neither of our fathers were active in our lives. So, I guess Miles was the only "daddy" available to settle for.

"Leaving? Where are you going, Mommy?" Rahmel asked with a saddened look of expression.

"Mommy is going into the army to make a better life for us all," she replied. Mother turned her head to face Rahmel with a smile, who was sitting directly behind her in the backseat.

"For how long?" Rodney asked with a sullen voice and a worried look on his face. He did not express it but our mother leaving would surely shift more responsibility on to him as our big brother.

69

"Well, my full contract is for four years but I will be able to come home for breaks in between. Whenever I have time off, I will be home with y'all. We will talk every day, we will write letters, everything will be fine, Rodney," Mother tried to persuade us all, including herself.

There was silence for a minute, but it seemed like forever. I could not believe what I had just heard. She was leaving us and, I just did not understand.

"Ma, where are we going to live? Who will look after us for all that time you will be gone?" I asked.

She did not smile at my question. Instead, she did offer a stern stare through the rear-view mirror, followed by the rolling of her eyes. Mother then turned her head towards the passenger seat where I was sitting.

"What do you mean where will you live, Rasheedah? What type of stupid question is that? Where do you live now?" she barked. "Y'all will continue to live at the apartment with daddy. When he is working, and when y'all are not at school, he says his family has offered to help look after y'all while I am gone," she spoke with agitation.

The world stood still. I froze and began to feel nauseated. My mind drifted off into space as I pondered over the trouble ahead. As Mother continued to speak, I could not hear her, she may as well have been speaking another language. It was all gibberish except for "his family has offered to help look after y'all". 'Oh no God please,' I silently pleaded without moving my lips.

"Why can't we just go along with you?" I blurted out.

"Rasheedah, because children are not allowed, and because I said so," she said.

I kept quiet. Not because I didn't have anything to say but mainly because I was thinking of where I could go. Who could I stay with for the duration of Mother's time in the army?

"Ma, can I go stay with aunt Piggy? I don't want to go over Samuel's house," I asked.

Rodney looked at me relieved that I had said the words that he too wanted to say.

"I don't give a fuck what your black ass wants! You got too much mouth and I am sick of hearing it so shut the fuck up," she ordered.

"I was just asking a simple question," I pouted.

"Rasheedah zip your fucking lips, girl!" Mother yelled.

And so, I did.

I Want to Go Home

"Ohhh yes! Yes, yesssss! Here it comes, I'm coming, I'm coming, I am coming!" Timothy screamed as he collapsed his sweaty naked body atop of me panting uncontrollably.

I squirmed and grunted trying to adjust to his stocky teenage body squishing my tiny body.

"Shut the fuck up," he said trying to catch his breath. "You better be lucky your pussy is so good," he said removing his limp penis from the inside of me. "I can't get enough of it."

I remained silent.

"Now go wash up," he demanded as he usually does once he was finished.

I stood to do as I was told when his bedroom door opened.

"What y'all in here doing!" Randy yelled, startling Timothy and me. He stared with a look of shock. "Ooh Oooh, I am telling on y'all," he threatened as he walked in and closed the door. "I am telling," he exclaimed.

Timothy did not seem worried whatsoever, "you ain't telling shit! Her ugly ass begged for it," he blatantly told a bald-faced lie.

I began to cry fearfully that Miles's other brother Randy was going to tell Samuel that I had done something wrong.

"Shut the fuck up! Shut up, Rasheedah!" Timothy shouted as he threw my t-shirt at me, summoning me to cover up my oversized breasts.

"No, don't cover them shits up," Randy spoke with a devilish grin.

"Them shits look good don't they? They are big as hell!" Timothy smiled as he touched one of my breasts.

"Yeah, they making my dick hard as fuck," Randy said rubbing the bulge in his pants.

"I'll let you have some of that dark chocolate if you keep your mouth closed," Timothy said looking at Randy.

I began to cry, again.

"Girl, shut up!" Randy said. "I don't want none of that burnt pussy," he laughed. Timothy joined in.

"You sure? It is really good," Timothy asked Randy as if he was offering him a glass of water.

"Nah, I don't want to fuck her, but I will let her suck my dick," he said as he removed a swelled penis from his windbreaker pants.

"Fine with me. I'll let y'all have some privacy then. And don't nut in her mouth or she'll throw up on you, trust me I know," Timothy winked at his brother and then exited the bedroom.

*

Mother had been gone a little over five months before I finally had had enough of the painful experiences that synchronized with Miles dropping us off at his father's house before heading to be with Yvette and Kristin. I ran away for the first time and was gone for hours before a patrol officer located me on Central Avenue, a busy shopping district within the city limits of East Orange.

"Young lady, why are you out late at night alone? What is your name sweetheart?" the young officer kindly asked. He seemed nice but I trusted no one, so I ran as fast as I could. He got into his car and followed me until I ran out of breath and stopped running.

He got out of the patrol car and walked alongside me when another police car pulled up. I began screaming as I thought I was in trouble for what I was doing with Timothy and Randy. They had forced me to do those nasty things countless times but yet I was the one getting into trouble. I screamed even louder for help. "Help! Help! Help! I did nothing wrong!" I screamed as loud as I could.

"Calm down young lady, keep calm. We are here to help you. Stop screaming," the officer said trying to ease my fear. A female officer exited the second police car and walked other to the officer and me.

"What's your name, honey? How old are you?" she asked.

"Rasheedah," I replied lowering my head as I tried to control my huffing and puffing. "I am eight years old."

"This is our runaway," the female officer said speaking to the male officer.

"What's wrong, Rasheedah? Is everything okay? You can trust me. I am here to help you" the officer asked.

"I want to go home," I said through weeping eyes.

Face Everything and Recover

"Rasheedah, I want you to recognize your own strength. Well, let me rephrase that. Rasheedah, it is my hope that you feel empowered by all that you have survived and feel liberated in your ability to share your truth. I applaud you for having the audacity to stand in your truth. It takes guts and you are doing an amazing job. Me saying that is not to patronize you but to acknowledge how tough it can be to reveal one's skeletons. We all have low points in life but standing in our own truth restores our power to overcome those traumatic experiences in life. Do you need to take a break?" Isaiah asked looking at me as I struggled to control my emotions.

"No," I said flatly trying to maintain composure but failing miserably.

"It is always important to allow ourselves to experience the emotions that we feel at the moment we are feeling it. Do you get what I mean?" asked Isaiah.

I shook my head yes.

"Rasheedah, if you want to cry, cry. If you want to scream, scream. If you want to punch something, use the pillow beside you," Isaiah motioned for me to grab one of the hunter green accent pillows propped in tandem alongside me on the sofa. "Face your emotions, do not suppress them. That is how you free yourself from pain, you must face it. Give me feedback on what you are feeling right now in this very moment."

"Ashamed, hurt, weak, embarrassed," I said grabbing the box of Kleenex to blow my nose.

"You have every right to feel that way. I understand you feeling hurt. But can you elaborate on what about these traumatic experiences causes you to feel ashamed, weak, and embarrassed?" Isaiah asked.

"Here I am one year shy of being forty-years-old crying about what occurred over thirty years ago. I hate that I have not gotten over this. I hate that I am still haunted as if this just happened. And I have never spoken much about this in this great of detail because I hate to be overtaken with emotion about anything. So, to be this emotional is a sign of weakness for me and it is embarrassing," I replied.

"This happened over thirty years ago but you have never faced it, you have been running all of this time. Unfortunately, it will continue to haunt you until you stop avoiding dealing with it and managing your emotions accordingly. Have you ever heard of the acronym F.E.A.R? From the perspective of healing from trauma, myself and many of my colleagues in the field encourage our clients to apply F.E.A.R and that is to Face Everything And Recover. Similarly, to what I just encouraged you to do. If you want to cry, let it out, or if you…"

"What if you are angry? How do you process rage?" I asked.

"When it comes to any emotion that may arise the goal is to move mindfully. You have to be intentional in your purpose to face what you are feeling. For example, rage can cause some people to act irrationally or without regard if it is not mindfully addressed. A healthy way to channeling rage constructively is to recognize what triggered the rage in the first place. Be conscious of what brought you there and change your environment if that is an option. Another way to process rage is to take a series of deep breaths through your nose, and then exhaling through your mouth. That will immediately help to calm your body. I encourage you to practice taking deep breaths, not just as it relates to healing from the past, but in dealing with any stressful scenario.

Let's see what else…some people release rage through working out. Going for a walk, or any form of safe physical exercise. Others may choose to pray or profess a positive outcome over the circumstance. What are some ways that have helped you to deal with any stressful situation?" Isaiah asked.

"Listening to music is comforting but most times I write when I have things on my mind," I said.

"Writing is an excellent way to release bottled-up emotions. What are some things you've written?" Isaiah asked.

"I have dozens of journals that I have written in over the years. This one that I have brought with me tonight is of poems that I have written, and I have never shared them with anyone. I mainly write to clear my head, not for an audience or anything," I spoke softly while looking down at the floor.

"Rasheedah, if you are comfortable, I would like to hear your poems. I understand that it may be challenging to be vulnerable, but it could be a benefit in helping develop the most effective treatment plan in helping you heal. It is totally up to you," Isaiah said.

Before we do that, allow me to provide some more clinical feedback regarding the sexual violence that you have endured. Unfortunately, sex abuse is far more common than anyone would like to admit. At the national level, I think the stats report that one in every five girls will be a victim. And for the record let's be clear, you have nothing at all to be ashamed of. You mentioned that you felt that you had done something wrong but there is no way an eight, nine, ten, or eleven-year-old, or for any child to give consent to any adult. I am referring to these young men as adults because if your mother had ever pressed charges against them, Randy and Timothy were old enough to be tried as adults.

There are many types of sexual abuse. Some of the types are inappropriate sexual contact, which involves non-penetrating touching. Then there's incestuous sexual contact, child molestation, and the obvious sexual assault which involves physical penetration including rape. In your case, you have experienced all of the types, except for incestuous sex contact. Well, actually I take that back. The two men weren't your blood relatives but were technically considered to be family members given that your mother was married to their brother," Isaiah added.

"They are not the only family members," I mumbled.

"Pardon, what was that?" he asked not fully understanding my muffled voice.

Clearing my throat, I spoke with clarity, "I said Timothy and Randy were not the only ones that did sexual things to me. My mother would leave us with so-called family all the time. And more bad things would happen on the regular basis," I said.

"Who were the others?" Isaiah asked.

"My older female cousins on my mother's side of the family. Yes, it happened but it was nowhere near as worse as the hell Randy and Timothy put me through. Well actually," I said stopping myself.

"Well actually, what?" he asked. "Go ahead and finish your statement, it is okay. This is a safe, judgment-free zone," he persuaded.

"I was going to say that it was actually not as devastating as the horrible experiences with Randy and Timothy because it was less mentally and physically brutal. I know that sounds like I am justifying what occurred, but I am not. All I am saying is that I was not violently hurt, nor was I verbally ridiculed. I was not attacked. They performed oral sex on me and made me suck on their breasts. That was all that happened," I said.

"Did they ever make you perform oral sex on them? How long did this go on?" he asked back-to-back.

"No, they did not. It only happened a few times. I was twelve or thirteen-years-old," I said.

"Rasheedah, do not defend them or minimize what occurred?" he blurted. "Regardless, if it was less physically painful as the occurrences with Randy and Timothy, it was still inappropriate and is still sexual assault. "Did this happen around the same time that Randy and Timothy did what they did?"

"I am not at all defending them. It happened a few times after Mother's breakup with Miles. When Mother and Miles finally split for good, she hardly ever spent any time with us, she never stayed home. She ran the streets a lot. The evenings that she would entertain men at the apartment, Mother would drop us off at one of her sibling's houses. The situation with my female cousins happened at my uncle's house. Two of my uncle's daughters would get sexual sometimes when we would go there," I said. "The last therapist tried to associate my sexuality with being molested by my female cousins. I ask that you not go there, please," I said with frustration.

"Why is that? Do you think that your history is connected to your sexuality?" Isaiah questioned.

"Hell no!" I said revealing my annoyance.

"Your position is well taken. Let me ask you this, do you identify as a lesbian?" Isaiah asked.

"I identify as Rasheedah Taylor. I have never categorized my sexuality because I have dated men and women since high school. While I have had multiple relationships with men and even am currently married to a great man whom I truly love, I have never had an unassisted orgasm with any man that I have ever been with, husband included. Most importantly, I have never felt as strong of an intimate connection with a guy that I have ever been intimately involved with like I have with women.

When it comes to sexuality, I knew early on that I was attracted to girls but was fearful of my attraction, so I mastered suppressing my feelings. My entire life I was taught that being gay was an act of evil, an abomination by many of my homophobic family members. Meanwhile, one of the people condemning how horrible homosexuality was also enjoyed licking my pussy every opportunity she got. So, there you have it, hypocrisy at the front directly in the center" I sarcastically exclaimed.

"But to be completely honest, I don't know if the sexual abuse has anything to do with my preference of attraction. I can tell you this, my first crush was a woman. Her name was Miss Turner, and she was the teacher's assistant in my first-grade class. Miss Turner was so fine! I would write her love letters and bring in snacks to get her attention," I giggled like a schoolgirl. "I even told Miss Turner that I want to marry her because she is so beautiful. She laughed it off but never mistreated me for making such a statement. Anyway, for many years I struggled with my attraction for women. I never publicized it but did discreetly date women as early as my high school years," I said.

"If you have always connected more with women, then why were you involved with men at all?" Isaiah asked.

"Sad to say but truthfully speaking, it's because it is what I was taught was the normal thing to do. I was afraid to do otherwise. While my husband, Warren and I share a deep love, I must admit that my desires for women have never ceased. The level of my attraction for women has endured. Even now after so much time has passed. I have been married to Warren for over ten years now," I said.

"Have you ever acted on those desires during your marriage?" he asked.

"No, and that is simply because I am monogamous and devoted to the man, I committed my life until death does us part. In the past, I would try to conceal how appealing I found women to be because it was very uncommon for anyone to admit they were attracted to the same sex at that time. So, I would be with girls in secret. I was a very shy person, very guarded. And so, I would be with girls who would pursue me, and we would discreetly be intimately involved," I admitted.

83

"While there have been ongoing studies on the impact of sex abuse on sexual identity, the results are inconclusive.

Some researchers have reported that sexual abuse can be an underlying cause for someone to be a homosexual, other researchers have challenged that theory. What do you believe?" he asked.

"I don't know the science or what's behind this notion, but it does bother me that anyone would make such a generalized statement by assuming every gay person has been abused. While that may be the case for some, it is not definitive in every situation. Therefore, it is irresponsible to jump to conclusions. The circumstances that I was faced with discredits the theory because I was sexually abused by males and females. So, if the research were accurate, wouldn't I be asexual?" I awkwardly laughed at my own dry joke.

"But seriously, that just seems absolutely ridiculous! If that were the case, I never would have been involved with men at all given the brutal sexual violence I endured most of my childhood and certainly would not be happily married to Warren. To me, one thing has nothing to do with the other," I projected.

"It is noteworthy to mention that there are emerging studies that also suggest how exposure to sexual abuse is linked to hypersexuality. Hypersexuality or a highly sexually active person is nonexclusive to heterosexuals or homosexuals. These theories are all undetermined. And for just as many upholding this data, there are just as many theorists dispelling the data," Isaiah said.

"There definitely were moments in my life when I was promiscuous. It is something that I am not at all proud of. I have learned from my mistakes and feel ashamed for not recognizing that I am of value," I said shamefully shaking my head. "This was happening around the same time Mother came back from the army and pretty much through my adolescence. I wanted acceptance, I wanted to be liked, and to feel loved, to feel worthy. To feel pretty, something that seemed so far from within my reach. Yet, all I was doing was allowing myself to be used. Giving myself away never made me feel any better. I still did not feel good enough," I sighed.

"We need to move on! This is far too painful to keep talking about" I yelled. "This is so hard! Even as a forty-year-old woman, I cannot face the past. The more I think about it, the more disturbed I become. I was a fucking child! A lost child with no guidance, just pure recklessness! I had no idea what I was doing. Not even cognizant of what sex was yet for these things to happen, I hate that I remember it. For years, I hated how I looked. Imagine having these large adult woman titties on a scrawny petite framed child. I just looked and felt awkward. Girls and boys took notice of my boobs, and many of them either made fun of me or wanted to squeeze them. And when I would say no, they would do it anyway and then they would still ridicule me. Can we stop here?" I grew angry. "I am so mad at myself for crumbling in front of you. Speaking about this stirs up so much emotion. My life was hell! I hated my appearance. My breasts were a curse and they kept getting bigger and bigger. By the time I was in junior high school I was a double D-cup and I got even more of the wrong attention.

One day I was walking home from school and was followed by a grown man. He kept asking me to stop and talk with him but I kept walking. He continued to follow me so I began to run. I ran as fast as I could until I finally made it home. I told my mom and stepdad about it. My stepdad insisted that we notify the police. A couple of days later I was walking home and the same thing happened again. This time the man was riding a bicycle and the police arrested him. This was life for me. One day I recall going into the garage and stealing my stepdad's duct tape. I duct taped my titties down until I was completely flat-chested. It hurt like hell removing the tape every night but I did not care, I got tired of being teased. That solution worked for a while until the adhesive from the tape made areas of my breasts raw and infected," I said.

"Did your mother ever notice what you were doing? If so, what was her reaction?" Isaiah asked.

"She knew I was doing it and even tried helping me try to shrink my boobs," I said.

Isaiah stared at me with a bewildered look of confusion, "How do you mean?" he asked.

"Mother said that she used to have the same issue and to shrink her boobs, she used camphor oil to dry up her breast tissue. Despite having applied it to my breasts twice a day, in the morning and at bedtime, the oil never helped to shrink my breasts. I was pissed because that oil smelled horrible, it had a strong menthol odor. All of that effort and the shit didn't work! Finally, at the age of seventeen, I underwent breast reduction surgery. It was the best thing I could have ever done," I said exhaling as I thought of the journey traveled.

"I am so sorry you felt that you needed to do something that drastic simply to avoid the attention you received from others. That is unfortunate, Rasheedah," he said.

"As I was explaining, while there are studies that show promiscuity and hypersexuality as potential side effects of sexual trauma, it is not definitive. It is completely reversible and something that is within your ability to change, whereas the sexual trauma that you experienced, was not within your control. In life, the things we can change, we change. You have nothing to be ashamed of, just learn from it and evolve from those types of destructive behaviors," he said.

"Isaiah, I keep trying to block it out, I keep trying to forget but I can't. I have been to hell and back. Sexual exploitation became so routine that I did not realize it was wrong. As a kid, I rationalized it was supposed to happen," I said.

"It is not uncommon…" Isaiah said.

"I would like to stop. If it is okay, I would like to end with one of my journal entries before I go," I cut him off.

"That is fine. I completely understand. Let's end with the poem," Isaiah spoke softly.

F.E.A.R. YOUR SANITY

Dark and Ugly

Ugly! Blackie! Big Teeth Bitch! Whoopi! I was all these things but yet you stole my innocence. Robbed me of any healthy self-esteem. Your words hurt me more than the physical sex pain. I was a child your assaults and verbal slayings changes my life forever, never will I be the same

Slaughtered possibilities of positive self-perception coinciding with your erections were outburst of additional hurt. Calling me horrible names made the experience much worse. Didn't know it then but these attacks made my soul cry. You convincing me that you were doing me a favor because nobody wanted me, so yes at the age of 10 I wanted to die. Taking Advil from the cabinet drawer I swallowed them all hoping to permanently close my eyes.

Your actions made me feel ugly and unworthy to live. What had I done to deserve this? I was just a kid. Self-hatred consumed my existence, remains to be an ongoing battle I am faced with today. I blamed myself for being overdeveloped, not pretty enough. So that's why I deserved your treating me that way.

Black skin, Big teeth, Big titties. For years I hated God for allowing this to be. How could God allow this to happen if he really loved me? My letters to Him were specific in detail. Change me, make me pretty but he never answered to no avail. I would write but He never replied. Where is this almighty God?

I would write, was He even listening? Change my skin God. If you love me, you will make me light skin. Take away my big chest, reinvent me. Take away my big teeth. It hurts that everyone makes fun of me. Make me pretty God so that he won't keep touching my body. He said I should be happy because I'm black as midnight and he was doing it to me. God if you are up there, please make my dreams reality.

Change me overnight so that I may awake happy. Countless letters, consistent disappointment. I grew to hate everyone, including myself. You continued to invade me physically and mentally, no one was there to help. Fear and anxiety from harm. Major challenges I have yet to overcome. Nighttime horrors forced me not to trust people.

F.E.A.R. YOUR SANITY

Literally became a loner, a prisoner to confinement. Permanent scars on my heart. Does it even matter to you that up until the age of nineteen, I was afraid to sleep in the dark?

Afraid to leave my room at night, or to even to open the door. Shameful to admit but instead of going to the bathroom I would piss in the corner, in the bed or on my bedroom floor.

Haunted by what you did to me. While this happened so long ago, it will forever live in my memory.

Face Everything and Recover Your Sanity

"Very productive session, Rasheedah. You did very well," Isaiah reassured. "One last thing. Give me a number on a scale of 1 to 10 that describes your mental state of mind right now."

"Maybe an 8. It may be hard to believe but I honestly feel some relief. My mental state was a 10 before we began this evening. I thought reading the poem would draw out more emotion, but it made me feel better. I am coming from a place of worry and fear. I have indeed tried to outrun my past but after running for so long, I am tired. Especially knowing that it has not gotten me anywhere. I want to heal. Pretending all of these years that I am okay has kept me in bondage. I now realize that it is where I will remain if I do not conquer the horrors of my past. If there is a way to improve, I know it is worth a try. I am also aware that it is uncommon for black people to seek professional help for their mental state," I smirked, "but I really need it."

"Yes, it is taboo in the black community to acknowledge mental illness. The stigma associated with seeking help for distress is why so many people within our community suffer in silence, self-medicate by turning to other destructive vices such as alcoholism or even drug abuse. Unfortunately, many never seek help and some end up committing suicide. So, I am very proud of you Rasheedah. Stay the course," he encouraged.

"I will. At the next session, I would like it if we can continue with the same structure as today. I will finish up my experiences of trauma. Then we can take on my destructive experiences that I believe result from unresolved trauma. Last will be perseverance, and restoration. Although I have been through some rough things, it has not been all bad. It ain't all good, either, but I have overcome so much in my life," I proudly said.

"Nothing is ever all good or all bad for that matter. No one is exempt from the ups and downs of life. What matters is how we navigate through life experiences while maintaining our sanity. Despite what you have gone through, you have managed to navigate the ship without allowing it to sink. You are still standing, Rasheedah. You have not let your experiences stop you from thriving. So, from that lens, you have always been on a path of recovery. I will help you to F.E.A.R. and that is to Face Everything And Recover for your overall well-being and sanity," Isaiah smiled. "We will change the idea of what FEAR actually is. Together we will rebuild, we will transform all of that pain you have endured into purposeful power. You are stronger than you know, but you just have to tap into that strength by recovering what's been broken for so many years," Isaiah said with enthusiasm.

"I have lived this way my entire life, so this newfound life you speak of does not feel attainable to me just yet. However, I dream of an unimaginable life where all of the layers of pain, shame, dismay, hurt, rejection, abandonment, and unworthiness are stripped away. Therapy has renewed my hope for better days ahead. Indeed, the hard things have come before all of the good things. Have a nice evening Isaiah, I will see you next time," I smiled and walked out of his office.

Home Alone

Mother returned to East Orange, New Jersey after serving four years in the military. A lot had happened during those four years for her as well as for us. She returned completely different and the three of us had undergone our own changes. I was twelve, my brothers Rodney and Rahmel were sixteen and eight years old. While still considered young kids, those four years away from Mother forced us to mature a lot sooner than normal kids our age.

For the first two and a half years of Mother's time in the military, my brothers and I spent most of our time with Miles's family. He justified this by claiming he was working overtime and wanted us to have fun by being around other kids. Miles would drop us off and pay Samuel a few dollars to allow us to stay overnight. During these visits, I experienced physical, mental, and violent sexual abuse on an ongoing basis the entire time Mother was gone. The physical abuse started after several runaway attempts. It was a horrible experience, to say the least, and it shaped me forever. The dreadful experience resulted in me going from being a bold, inquisitive, and talkative child to being a quiet, bashful, and angry child. No longer looking directly into anyone's eyes, I often isolated myself with the intent of being left alone. Whenever I did speak to anyone, including my brothers, I was hostile and irate. I had already gotten used to being called all kinds of names for as long as I could remember so adding "mean" or "rude" or

94

"crazy" to the list had less of an impact. The evolution of my unpleasant aura created dissension amongst everyone I encountered and that was fine with me. The discord was for my safety. I was sick and tired of being in pain, so I had taken matters into my own hands since there was no one around to save me from harm.

Timothy and Randy would take turns coming into the den or spare bedroom where I slept. They were much older than us, so we never objected to our sleeping assignments in "their house" out of fear of verbal assaults or the embarrassment of being thrown out in the middle of the night. My brothers hated being at Samuel's house just as much as I did but we felt defenseless.

Despite, the recent changes in my relationship with my brothers, they still did not like Samuel's kids calling me names. Whenever my brothers were around for the name-calling, they would often speak up for me which resulted in them being punched or called names.

As time went on, I began having nightmares or sometimes, I could not sleep at all. I would stay awake watching the door, hoping that Timothy or Randy would have mercy on me and leave me the fuck alone. The likelihood of them not walking through the door was very slim so I stayed awake waiting for it to happen. I began wetting the bed or peeing on myself to avoid walking to the bathroom. I was so afraid of who was behind the door, so I stayed put. After a while of wetting the bed or sofa, Samuel banned us from coming over to his house.

"Rasheedah's nasty ass pissed in the bed, again! And this time will be her last time. Miles, I tried to be of help to you but, keep them bastards home. They can't come back here," Samuel yelled when Miles picked us up one day during our final visit. It was the greatest thing that could ever happen.

"Goddamn it, Rasheeda!" Miles yelled as we walked to his car. "I cannot wait for your mother to bring her ass back here! It is always you! One minute you pissing on the floor at home now you have graduated to pissing in beds now?" he asked.

"I'm sorry," I said somberly.

"Sorry for what? Why can't you just get up and go to the bathroom like you always used to? I don't understand it, Rasheeda I really don't understand," Miles said softening his approach. "What is it, is it because you miss Sandra?" he asked.

I shook my head. "No, I am just scared to walk to the bathroom in the dark," I admitted.

"Don't be afraid of the dark. Just cut on the light Rasheeda, that is all. Nobody is going to hurt you," he continued unaware of my reality.

If only what Miles was saying stood to be true. Everything changed for me after the molestation started especially how I socially interacted with others. However, never being welcome back to Samuel's house made me so happy. I knew that I would be safer at home.

Miles drove us back home and that is where we remained, just the three of us for the most part. My brothers and I ended up staying in our small Halsted Street apartment alone for days at a time. We hardly ever saw Miles. It was the best feeling to be together again in our own home, with nobody hurting or yelling obscenities at us. Rodney was such a great big brother because he got us on a schedule. He and I worked as a team to take care of Rahmel. We would awake, get dressed for school and Rodney would walk us to our respective schools, and then he would walk to school. All three of us attended different schools given the four-year age differences between us. After school, I would make food for us. I learned how to cook very well as a means of survival for my brothers and me. Whenever we did not have microwave-friendly foods available, I began thawing meat from the freezer and cooking full meals on the stovetop or in the oven. Despite the normalcy I tried to create, I became a person in constant fear. Every day I grew worried that Samuel would change his mind and extend the offer to give Miles a break by allowing us to come back over to play with the other kids in the neighborhood.

*

Upon Mother's return from active duty, Miles finally admitted to her that the marriage was over and that he was leaving Mother for Yvette. Mother was not surprised because Miles had already moved all of his belongings out of our apartment and in with Yvette. When Mother returned, she asked us "how often did Miles stay here in this apartment with y'all"?

"Mommy we would see Miles a few days out the week," Rodney lied to lessen the blow. I would typically intervene by blurting out the truth but this time I remained silent. I had learned to keep quiet and so I did.

"Well, I am home now, and never will I leave y'all again," Mother said kissing Rodney on the cheek and then embracing him as Rahmel ran over to join in on the group hug. I sat on the worn sofa staring in disgust at them hugging the woman who had left us for years in an unsafe environment. I could not believe what I was seeing and wondered in my mind what the hell was wrong with my brothers. Rodney and Rahmel were happy to see Mother, the same person that abandoned us like we did not mean anything to her. The same woman who left us to fend for ourselves, and who endangered our lives by leaving us with people who physically and sexually abused us. I could not understand it.

"Rasheedah, come over here and hug your mother. Didn't you miss me"? she asked.

"I guess," I lied. Of course, I missed her more than she would ever know. I went over to join my brothers in hugging our mother. I hugged her neck so tight and would not let go.

The next thing I knew, my brothers were rubbing my back, "it's okay Rasheedah." They had stopped hugging Mother and were now hugging me.

"What's the matter, Rasheedah?" Mother asked while hugging me, too.

"I am safe now," I screamed. "I am safe now." I screamed again as I bawled my eyes out and continued tightly hugging our mother. For once I felt comfort and concern from her. Typically, Mother was not the emotional type when it came to crying or even expressing herself, but it was clear that the separation had taken a toll on us all.

"I have missed you all so much, you have no idea," Mother said.

"Mommy, we missed you too," I said beating my brothers to the punch. "I am so sorry for being bad all those other times. I'm going to be good forever now, Mommy," I jumped into her arms hugging her again.

"Girl what are you doing? You really are showing a different side of yourself. You really must have missed me," Mother laughed.

I shook my head in agreement. I never said anything about what Timothy and Randy had done at that time. In my mind, everything would be okay now that I no longer had to go over there. My goal was to put all of the horrible things I had done behind me.

Rage

The dissolution of Mother's marriage to Miles was liberating for my brothers and me but even for her, too. Upon settling in from the army, Mother secured an administrative job within the pharmaceutical industry and moved on with her life fast. She was an attractive caramel woman whose 5-foot-8-inch athletic frame had only improved during her time in the army. Mother had a figure-eight shape and was a desirable woman. She never had trouble getting attention from men, she dated whomever she wanted. So, with Miles being gone from her life, Mother juggled dating several men at one time.

Everything changed, including Mother reconnecting with family members who detached themselves due to her relationship with Miles. Mother's side of the family was reintroduced back into our lives because no one on her side of the family was supportive of her marriage to Miles. Everyone was receptive to her announcement of separating from her husband, especially our aunt, Debra, whom we called Piggy. Having everyone's approval to move on with her life gave Mother ammunition to continue to serial date. After working her normal day shift, Mother would hit the streets. She partied on the regular basis and would come home in the middle of the night during the weekdays. On the weekends Mother would always stay out overnight. Sometimes aunt Piggy would come to stay with us on the weekends, along with our cousin Andre, when Mother would complain of 'needing a break' from being a single mom. On the days that Piggy was unavailable to stay over, it was just my brothers and me, and I was fine with that. We all had gotten used to being home alone. However, after a while Mother's nights out became excessive. She was relentless in conducting herself in a manner that suggested she had no children. She was never in the home and when she was, Mother was disengaged. The three of us were self-sufficient. We had already established a routine while Mother was away so we hardly ever relied on her to help with simple things such as homework, bathing, getting ready for school the next day, or preparing dinner. We'd learned to survive without her because we had no choice.

One Sunday morning Mother arrived home, after having spent the entire weekend out, with two dozen of Dunkin Donuts. My brothers and I were congregating in our usual places, which were on the sofa or on the floor in front of the coffee table in the living room watching Hot to Trot when we heard keys jingling at the front door. Mother appeared with the neon pink and orange boxes as she announced, "kids I am home!" My brothers were ecstatic and began enacting their usual routine which involved them running to the door to greet our mother with hugs and kisses. I stubbornly remained planted on the sofa as they followed her into the kitchen.

"I got y'all something," she excitedly announced as she placed the donuts on the glass kitchen table.

"Aww, thanks Mommy!" the boys said gleefully.

I was infuriated and fed up with my brothers giving our mother a pass for her irresponsibility and lack of regard for our safety. The pattern had become too routine. Mother would go missing for two or three days, return with some sort of goodies, my brothers would be thrilled, and I would be pissed. Then days later the pattern would repeat all over again.

"Rodney and Rahmel y'all both are so stupid!" I frowned looking at them with disgust.

"Shut up Rasheedah and come have a donut before me and Scooby eat them all up," Rahmel teased offering me a donut in between bites. "Mommy, these donuts are so good," he continued to patronize her.

"I am glad you are enjoying them, my handsome big boy," Mother said.

The pseudo affection was unbearable and was sickening to watch.

"Oh my God! Did y'all forget that we have not seen our mother since Friday morning before we went to school? Y'all are so stupid, I swear to God. All it takes for y'all to forgive her for leaving us again in this house for three days are some stale donuts. Stupid dummies, no thank you," I spat with fury.

"Bitch, you need to shut the fuck up! You are the kid, and I am the adult," Mother exclaimed. I'd usually recalibrate my tone by now but this time my frustration took over.

"You don't care nothing about us. We don't even have any food in this house and you have been gone for days. What kind of mother does that to her own kids," I yelled back.

"If you don't like it, there is the door bitch. And if you keep talking shit I am gonna whoop your monkey ass," Mother stood in the living room doorway exposing her fuchsia satin gown under her white knit shirt.

"I wish I could go live with my father," I said not knowing exactly who the hell my father was since I'd never met him but it sounded good when I blurted it out.

"Girl, your ugly ass father don't want to be bothered with your black ass and neither do I! You get on my muthafucking nerves," Mother said as she walked towards her bedroom. "And you better not eat not one of those donuts bitch," she yelled before slamming her bedroom door closed.

I don't want none of them nasty ass donuts, bitch! I quietly mumbled under my breath. While I loved my Mother, I resented her for hardly ever being present in our lives. Out of the three of us, Mother just did not seem to have any love for me in particular. When it came to Rodney and Rahmel, Mother always seemed nicer to them, and less kind to me. She always seemed disinterested and cold towards me. Despite many attempts to gain her attention and affection, Mother never was receptive. It seemed the more I pushed the harsher she became. Over time, I began to match her with the same level of disdain she had given me for as long as I could remember.

As far as I was concerned, I had every right to hate Mother. I blamed her for everything wrong in my life at that point including all of the physical, mental and sexual abuse I endured when she was home and while she was away serving in the military. Her absence was the cause of severe physical pain. Along with the pain, I was taunted and verbally attacked by the monsters responsible for stealing my innocence. I was a kid who was defenseless against grown-ass men who could not keep their hands off of me. I hated her for not being there for me when I needed her most. Her leaving us ruined my life and I simply could not pretend that all was well. Nothing about my childhood was well yet my mother did not seem to have any regrets because she continued to leave us alone once she returned from the army. She stayed away from the apartment and spent the night out all the time. She did not seem to care to spend any time with us and I resented my brothers for overlooking our mother's behavior.

As I grew older my disrespect and rage towards Mother worsened. We would get into arguments on the regular basis, often resulting in physical altercations. While I never would initiate a fight with Mother. However, I never backed down whenever she would start one. Mother often would slap or punch me, and defensively I would respond with verbal assaults on her character. One evening she had one of her male companions sleeping overnight and I scolded her while the man was there.

"You always have all these different men in and out around your kids," I said loud enough for the man to overhear me from Mother's bedroom.

"You little black bitch," Mother looked embarrassed. She slapped me across my face and attempted to drag me off of the floor by pulling the collar of my shirt. "I'm going to kill you," she said as she and I tussled back and forth.

"Get the fuck off of me, I hate you! Get your fucking hands off of me," I said fighting to break free but Mother refused to let me go. We continued to scuffle and cuss each other out.

"You little bitch! You think you are grown. I will show you what it is to take a grown woman ass-whooping since you want to be so disrespectful and bold," Mother said dragging me towards my bedroom.

"Get the fuck off of me hoe! Get your hands off of me, and leave me the fuck alone," I yelled as my brothers looked on angrily. With piercing eyes, Rodney chastised me, "Rasheedah, you need to shut up and stop talking to Mommy like she one of your little friends. Stop it right now," he exclaimed.

"That's right, stop it right now Rasheedah. Stop it right now! Leave my Mommy alone!" Rahmel cried.

"Well tell your Mother to stop bringing all these different men in here every other night!" I shouted defiantly as I continued to kick and scream obscenities.

Mother threw me into my room and slammed the door, "You keep your little black ass in this room and do not come out for a muthafucking thing! Do you hear me? You are not allowed out of that room for the rest of the night. Boys, y'all let me know if she brings her ass out that room," Mother said to Rodney and Rahmel.

From the inside of my bedroom, I kicked the door with force repeatedly.

"I hate your fucking guts, hoe ass! You are the worse mother in the world!" I screamed as the tears and snot streamed down my face. "I wish I had a different mother! Someone who is about something," I shouted.

"The feeling is mutual you nappy-headed bitch! I wish I had a different daughter and if you don't like living here, you are always welcome to get the fuck out at any time," Mother said closing the door behind her.

F.E.A.R. YOUR SANITY

Estranged

Years of pain
hurtful mistreatment
unlike the love shown for my brothers
never have I received the same treatment
Estranged
result of denial
haunted by a horrible past
efforts to minimize accountability
impact of brutal assaults will forever last
It can never be swept under the carpet
denial will never dismiss years of hardship
Cuts like a rusted knife
your own flesh and blood
the cause of such strife
zero acknowledgment of suffrage
leaves one to question where is the love?
Never once ever heard you say 'I love you daughter'
Even as a child, not a kiss or a hug
Deep dark pain
Not a fallacy
From childhood to adulthood
My harsh reality
Your unconcern of trauma stunts my recovery
years and years of forced sex
just a child, assaulted by those you trusted when you left
Your leaving us behind infuriates me
Your irresponsibility
Questions of what kind of mother would do something so crazy
Estranged
What can you do?
How about acknowledge the pain
Address the mistakes that led to this disdain
Accept responsibility, never not one apology
for permitting others to hurt me
Left to figure it out on my own
Hard knock life
Sexed up and beat down, words cannot describe the emptiness of
feeling so alone
Men coming into my room at night
A mother abandoning three kids, out having the time of her life
A child who would daydream to escape the pain

108

F.E.A.R. YOUR SANITY

Wishing things weren't as bad as it seemed
Screaming for help wishing someone would care
Looking for mama to return
Yet she never did, no one was there
How could I respect you now?
Truth is you were never around
I recollect a painful childhood that surely would have been different
had you been there
I sob myself to sleep angry asking God why, life never seemed fair
As a child everything is black and white, there are no shades of gray
Like it happened yesterday, I recall the bad times and always
wondered why you left us that way

It changed me forever if only you paid attention, took the time to see
Sex abuse constantly, verbal insults equate to a fucked up
psychological reality
Pains of the past will forever remain, the horrors won't fade, no
drug, no drink has ever made it go away
As an adult I live in a beautiful big house
on a fancy exclusive street
Pushing forward I have greatly achieved
yet when it comes to the past, it remains a bad dream
To this day there are still nights of no sleep
So, to deny my past enrages me, to dismiss it denies the fucked up
shit that happened to me
Growing older, with expectation to live a fallacy free of abandoning
your children, leaving one to be raped, beat, assaulted repeatedly
When you consider all of the above, it is really a damn shame
it is clear why we are estranged

F.E.A.R. YOUR SANITY

Hurt People Hurt People

The year was 1970 and it was a cold March snowy day as Sandra, Debra and Richard trekked through the snow heading home. The three were excited that the weekend had finally arrived. Although it was snowing heavily the three kids anxiously rushed home as they anticipated spending the weekend with their dad, Thomas. Every weekend was spent with their dad, the kids never tired from the visit as it was the only time they felt safe.

The kids arrived at the apartment that they shared with their mother and seven older siblings. Their mother, Betty Lynn, had given birth to ten children ranging from ages five-years-old to twenty-one-years old. The children had different fathers but Sandra, Debra, and Richard all shared the same father. They also were the youngest of Betty Lynn's ten children. Sandra was 8-years-old; Debra, affectionately known as Piggy, was 7-years-old, and Richard was 5-years-old.

The older siblings with the exception of Betty Lynn's firstborn, Clifford, all struggled with substance abuse. Several of them were in and out of prison, two of which had even given birth to their own children while incarcerated. Betty Lynn was also tasked with having to take care of her grandchildren while her daughters and sons ran the streets of Newark. Betty Lynn struggled to keep her youngest children fed and clothed, as it was routine for the older ones to steal food, money, and clothing from the apartment to feed their heroin addictions. So,

Sandra, Piggy, and Richard enjoyed spending the weekends with their daddy because they were confident they would have food to eat and a warm place to sleep.

As Sandra opened the door the children could hear shouting and laughter. They walked in and Ronald, David, Margaret, and Barbara, were at the kitchen table arguing over who was next. Once they finally could agree, there was anxious silence. Sandra walked over to the table to say hello.

"Hey, girl. Y'all are back so soon. Go on in the back with Mommy. Take Piggy and Richard with you," Sandra's older sister, Barbara ordered.

Sandra looked at the large bowl of bloodied water. Barbara had the belt affixed tightly around Ronald's arm. He anxiously awaited for his younger siblings to disappear into the back room. "Would y'all hurry the fuck out of here? I cannot wait any longer. Do me right now," Ronald shouted as he urged for Barbara to proceed with injecting the heroine into his vein.

"Come on y'all follow me," Sandra summoned for Piggy and Richard to follow her into their mother's room.

"Hey Mommy," they all greeted their mother as they entered her bedroom which felt as cold as an icebox. It was bone-chilling cold in the apartment since there was no heat. The heat had stopped working months ago. Given that Betty Lynn had not paid the rent in months, she could not contact the landlord to get help with fixing the problem.

Betty Lynn lay on the mattress wrapped in an oversized winter coat she had gotten from the Salvation Army at the start of the winter season. The mattress was flat on the floor with no box spring or bed frame underneath. When Betty Lynn heard her younger children running, she sat up and forced a smile onto her weary face.

"Hey, y'all. How are my babies, how was school?" their mother spoke with a heavy southern accent.

"School was ok. Mommy, I'm hungry. I only ate once today and that was at lunchtime," Richard replied. Betty Lynn sat motionless and stared off into a daze. She knew there was no food in the house. It was the middle of the month and she would not have any money until her food stamps replenished on the 1st of next month.

"Sandy, y'all get ready to walk over to Thomas's house. Y'all will eat once you get over there. He will have a couple of dollars and will get y'all something to eat," Betty Lynn said. Sandra quickly packed a bag for herself and her younger siblings and they prepared to leave.

"Ok, Mommy. We are leaving. We will see you when we get back on Sunday," Sandra said hugging her mother's neck tightly. Piggy and Richard followed her lead, "see you later Ma. We love you."

"All right, Sandy. You take care of your brother and sister. Look after them," Betty Lynn said looking at Sandra directly in her eyes.

112

"Ok I will, Ma," Sandra said as she, Piggy and Richard left their mother's room. They walked past the kitchen where their eldest siblings lay passed out at the table, and walked out of the front door.

They were thrilled to be away from the apartment for the weekend but had no idea that would be their last time seeing their mother for the next twenty years.

That Sunday evening Thomas drove the children back home only to find the door padlocked. Betty Lynn was nowhere to be found. They had no idea where their mother had gone and had no way of contacting her.

Months later Thomas learned that Betty Lynn's eldest son, Clifford had come home from the air force. When he arrived, he recognized the stress Betty Lynn had been under dealing with her older children's drug issues. Clifford's goal was to alleviate Betty Lynn from the struggles that plagued her due to the impact of his drug-addicted siblings. So, he packed up his mother's remaining belongings and drove Betty Lynn back down south to her hometown of Smithfield, North Carolina. It is there where Betty Lynn remained until her death some forty years later.

Sandra, Piggy, and Richard lived with their father Thomas until they reached their late teens. While Thomas was quite the disciplinarian and functional alcoholic, he did begrudgingly provide for his children by supplying them with food, shelter, and clothing. The three never forgave their mother, Betty Lynn, for leaving them behind. They felt that she had escaped to Smithfield and had forgotten about them. She never came back for her youngest three. The grudge upheld and their abandonment never was settled with their mother. At her funeral, which happened some forty years later, out of Betty Lynn's nine surviving children, Sandra, Piggy, and Richard were the only of her children that did not shed one tear at her memorial service.

The children resented Betty Lynn for her lack of regard for them. They appreciated that their dad was a provider to them when they were too young to care for themselves. However, love was absent from the equation. The children often felt to be a burden to Thomas who had been a bachelor all their lives leading up to Betty Lynn's departure, only seeing his children usually on the weekends. Despite all the trauma the three children had experienced, Sandra, Debra, and Richard persevered and learned to rely on one another for love, support, and protection. Sandra was more than a big sister to her younger siblings, she served more of a surrogate mother role in Debra and Richard's life. Over the years the three developed an unbreakable bond and remained distant from their other siblings.

Destruction* de·struc·tion | \ di-ˈstrək-shən (noun)

Definition of destruction

1: the state or fact of being destroyed : RUIN

2: the action or process of destroying something

3: a destroying agency

As defined by Merriam-Webster. (n.d.). Citation. In Merriam-Webster.com dictionary.
Retrieved January 15, 2021, from https://www.merriam-webster.com/dictionary/citation

On the Run

I lay there numb from the combination of the 151 cognac and the two Xanax pills I got from a classmate a day before. I was feeling good without worry. Toni Braxton filled the air with "Another Sad Love Song" as I drifted off and wondered what it was like to be as beautiful as the one and only Toni Braxton. She had it all: a curvy figure, a beautiful face, and a pretty honey complexion that men and women wanted. As my imagination and the euphoria of the liquor and pills concoction began to take control and liberate my mind to its true thoughts I began to tingle all over. I throbbed from within as I drifted far and imagined myself being wanted and admired by everyone who looked my way. The thought made me feel so damn sexy and so loved that I began to caress myself. The more she sang, the more I drifted into my own world imagining my own hands to be those of one of my admirers. Someone who loved me so much that they craved to be with me, craved to touch me, craved to look into my eyes pleading for me to feel the same way in return. As I glided my fingers in and out the feeling felt so genuine and so appeasing to be wanted. I was on the verge of climaxing when I heard the knob to my attic bedroom door open.

"Rasheedah!!" my mother screamed out of frustration.

"How many fucking times I have to call you before you answer me?" Sandra yelled.

Dazed from the booze and pills but especially angry because she robbed me of one hell of an orgasm, I gripped the comforter and went ballistic.

"Get out! I don't just storm into your room and start blasting on you! Get out!" I hollered as loud as I could.

"Rasheedah I have been calling you for the last five fucking minutes, what is so fucking hard about answering me when I call you?" she yelled back.

"Obviously I didn't hear you! I'm all the way up here in the attic and you expect me to hear you calling me. Wow, that's real smart," I answered as sarcastically as possible.

Disgusted by my attitude, my mother turned to walk out of my room.

Still in defense mode, I sat up and asked, "so what was so important for you to come all the way up here, only to turn around and leave?"

"We are about to leave for Virginia and Otis wanted to know if you were coming or not," she replied just as rude as she proceeded out the door before I could answer. She got halfway down the stairs when she shouted, "are you going or not!?"

Pissed because she could care less if I stayed or went along for the ride, I shouted out to her, "no!"

I jumped up and ran to the window to see if they were in the van. My mother was sitting in the passenger side sitting pretty as my southern and much older stepfather loaded up the

1995 Ford van. Otis was well over twenty-five years older than our mother.

I used to live for those long ass road trips with my stepfather until he started making it a priority for my mom to tag along. We were a family of five but my older brother, Rodney, and younger brother, Rahmel, did not enjoy road trips as much as I did. When Rodney was not away at college he hardly ever spent time with family. My youngest brother Rahmel didn't feel the need to go because our mother never forced him to do anything he did not have any interest in doing.

So that left me and my stepfather on the road at least two to three times a year. It was always an adventure. We would drive south to visit his relatives in a small town outside of Richmond, Virginia. I lived for those trips because although my stepfather lived in New Jersey the majority of his adult life, he was a southern man at heart and I loved him for that. He had a thick southern accent and a humble heart of gold. He was the only one of Mother's male companions who I had opened up to, and it was not on purpose. Otis was gentle and genuine to everyone who crossed his path that one couldn't help but open up and love him. He always seemed to care and I loved and respected him for that. He was the only man who ever cared enough to be a parent to me, Rodney, and Rahmel, even when our three daddies or mother didn't have the time or desire to.

F.E.A.R. YOUR SANITY

I bolted down the attic steps of our four-bedroom home with my car keys in hand en route to my weed man. As a young adult, my attitude was simple: I do not give a fuck. With exception to Otis, I was always under the perception that nobody gave two fucks about me, so I bestowed that same energy onto others. I felt like he cared because he always made a point to talk to me about life. Otis was never one to chastise but more so about educating me on the realities of life.

As I walked to my 1989 Ford Escort en route to cop, Otis watched me from his white conversion family van with sadness in his eyes. My mother, who was the epitome of materialistic physical perfection, sat oblivious to how high her only daughter was.

"Hey Rasheedah, come here let me talk to you," Otis said in a low southern undertone.

I walked to the van without shame only until he looked into my eyes. "Gal, come on and get in, we are going to Virginia. It'll wear off before we get to Cissy's house."

Before I could even respond, my mother interjected, "No! She already said she ain't going, now she needs to stay here! And Rasheedah, make sure my house is still standing when we get back. Make sure Rahmel doesn't have a houseful of his friends in my house either. Come on Otis, let's go!" Sandra prompted Otis to start up the ignition.

"Wait a minute Sandra, it's not on her to make sure Rahmel does the right thing by not having folks in the house.

You cannot keep expecting her to babysit him. That boy is nearly grown and should know better," said Otis.

"Look, y'all have a safe trip, I gotta go," I interjected attempting to defuse their disagreement.

Otis looked at me and said, "You sure you don't want to go? One of the reasons I was going this week is to show you some other colleges down in that area. We will pass a lot of black universities on the way down. Thought you wanted me to take you to Howard University. I keep telling you that is a great school Rasheedah. Plus, there's a lot of other schools to consider if you're not interested in that one. Maybe you can transfer there rather than commuting to Kean. You need to be away and living on campus to get the full experience of what college has to offer," he said.

Thrilled that he remembered one of our conversations about potentially going away to a black university I replied, "Nah, Otis, maybe some other time. I haven't decided if I'm going to apply to another college anyway, but thanks."

"Well gal, like I have always told you, never be afraid to explore all your options even if those options may require you to step outside of your comfort zone. Going away to school may be a better fit for you. Just think about it. Alright then, guess we will see you Sunday morning, we should be back by then," Otis said.

"Ok, see you later," I got in my car and pulled off before they could.

F.E.A.R. YOUR SANITY

As I drove I began to think about the look on my mother's face as Otis tried to convince me to take the road trip with them to Virginia. She always seemed to be so disgusted when it came to me. It was the, 'I don't give a fuck, you're interrupting me' look that she wore. The same look and mindset that I'd adapted to years before her meeting Otis, and years before she changed into the sophisticated and educated woman she had reinvented herself to be today.

In an instance, I was depressed and angry at the world. I hated my childhood and knew that it explained why I was so fucked up in the head. I trusted no one and hated and envied those who appeared to have had a normal life. My insecurities within myself and self-hatred were a direct reflection of my attitude towards others. I was not a people person. My unhappiness was imposed onto others by my rudeness and anger. I hated how I looked and was begrudging to those around me whose beauty I admired. Essentially, and as Mother often put it, "I was a bitch to the twenty-fifth power."

Before I knew it, I had copped a dime bag of weed and was on my way to Elmwood Park to smoke and drift like I was doing before I was so rudely interrupted by the wicked maternal witch. I stayed in the park for a few hours thinking. As I inhaled the smoke from the marijuana-filled cigar I immediately zoned out and allowed all my troubles to fade. I fell into a zone of comfort, but it was always a temporary solution. My mind was chaotic and always fixated on problems that I had no solutions for. One of those constant issues was my inability to shake a troubled past. No matter how often I intentionally tried to shut off my mind to escape, my troubles not only haunted me but consumed my mental space so much that I sometimes found it difficult to concentrate on anything else. The impact was so loud it was deafening. Then I would get mad at myself for losing the mental battle. It was suffering to want to rid myself of something but not knowing how.

As I sat back in my car, the horrible images of my childhood resurfaced creating a massive migraine on the left side of my head. Shit, here we go again I thought to myself. I needed an outlet fast, so I picked up the phone and called an old friend Bishop. Bishop was a former classmate and current fuck buddy. He and I use to attend the same high school until he had gotten expelled our junior year after his so-called friend informed school administrators that he brought a gun to school.

"What's good Chocolate?" Bishop answered on the first ring.

"Nothing, what's up with you?" I asked trying to redirect my attention from the horrible past to the present.

"This dick," he laughed.

"What?" I asked confused and still in pain from the migraine I was suffering from.

"You said "what's up" and I said, "this dick" now that you called me," he laughed at his own joke.

Sad but true. I only called Bishop when I was ready to fuck. I fucked only when my mind was someplace else which occurred more often than not. I was visiting Bishop at least five to six times a week to fuck until I forgot about whatever was bothering me.

"Look, I'm coming to see you. I'll be there in five minutes," I said before hanging up the phone.

I was at his house in less than five minutes being that he lived right around the corner from Elmwood Park.

Bishop was at the door before I got out of the car looking sexy and ready to beat it down.

He was a handsome man with caramel skin and shoulder-length dreads. Bishop was that dude in every sense of the word. He was six feet tall, stocky, and strong as hell. I would know because he often would pick up all 140-pounds of me and pound the shit out of me during sex. Bishop had this aggression about him that made me weak in the knees. Almost like an untouchable type of guy who shared my same philosophy, fuck the world. When I was with Bishop, we would get high and fuck like rabbits.

"I am starting to feel used. You just use the shit out of a brother," Bishop laughed revealing his beautiful white teeth.

"Oh please! Yeah whatever, you know you like that shit. Are you ready for round six?" I laughed with him while undressing him with my eyes.

"You damn right, for sure! Let's get it started then!" he smirked.

No words were spoken as he led me to his bedroom and closed the door behind us.

An hour later we lay next to one another listening to Whitney Houston's "You Give Good Love" on the quiet storm. I'm almost always quiet after sex. Not because I have nothing to say but mainly because I'm questioning why I keep fucking without purpose. I was always attracted to Bishop but more so in admiration of his popularity, swagger, and 'don't give a fuck attitude' rather than any intimate connection. It was going on two years that we had been seeing one another but still I felt like it was pointless. I only called him when I needed to alleviate heavy burdens off of my mind. It was routine for me to get depressed and drive over high out of my mind, get high again with him and then transition into how I always wanted to feel, beautiful and sexy. Without a doubt, Bishop always accomplished making me feel wanted, sexy and feminine with the aggression, confidence, and desire he would infuse on me. Sex with him always felt good and our connection was genuine at the same time. But it only worked for a moment because immediately afterward I went back to feeling used, unaccepted, misunderstood, and unpretty.

"Yo, why are you always so quiet after we fuck? And I know it's not because you didn't like it, I can tell you liked it

124

because you creamed all over my dick," he asked in a serious tone.

"I liked it, it's not that Bishop," I replied humbly.

"So, what is it Rasheedah?" he asked looking directly at me.

I raised up from the bed quickly so that he could not see the tears in my eyes. I don't know why but I always wanted him to think of me as tough as he was. I didn't want him to think of me as some attached thot who was clingy, so I played it cool.

"I just am thinking of how good daddy dick is, that's all!" I laughed as I stroked his ego.

"Did daddy tear it up, Chocolate or what? He asked already convinced that he knew the answer.

"Yes, Mr. Showtime! Let me give yo' ass a round of applause" I stood up and clapped my ass cheeks for him and we both erupted with laughter. I climbed on top of him and eventually, we dozed off in each other's arms.

A few hours later I woke up feeling sticky from his semen and groggy from the drugs that Bishop and I had taken before our evening of sex. He was still snoring when I jumped up frightened because all of the lights had been shut off. From day one, Bishop and I have always had sex with the lights on, and from day one he always questioned why I preferred to keep the lights on. I was always able to redirect the conversation by distracting him with oral sex to put an end to the uncomfortable questioning. My strategy seemed to work because Bishop would never bring it up until the next encounter.

I turned the light on and got dressed as fast as I could. Bishop awoke immediately after feeling me get up.

"What are you doing, why are you leaving?" Bishop asked sounding raspy and disgruntled.

"Because, Bishop, I have to get home to check on my brother. My mother told me to look after him while she's gone," I replied.

"Rasheedah, it's three o'clock in the fucking morning! Do not do this to me again. Listen, your little brother is not a baby. Either he is sleeping or in some pussy. Let that young dude live a little. Come back to bed with daddy, Chocolate," he stared trying to seduce me with his eyes.

I grew tensed as I was concerned that he was not buying my story, again. I jumped into defense mode to redirect his attention, "no, I'm not staying over here Bishop. What if your mother comes in here and catches us butt-ass naked?"

"Yo, what the fuck! My mom's ain't been an issue, so why now all of a sudden you bringing her up? She knows we be in here fucking, she already knows that you're a freak! Hell, she even heard you screaming one time!" he joked.

"You need to keep shit real and be honest. You don't want to stay all night because you don't want daddy to beat it up again. Just keep it real, you cannot handle another round," he commented with overconfidence.

I refused to explain why I could not spend the night with him. I was too embarrassed and too ashamed. So, to save

face and embarrassment, I once again, redirected the conversation and chose to pick an argument instead.

"Oh hell no, we ain't never fucked while Miss Johnson was here. So, who the fuck else you fucking because for damn sure it wasn't me!" I lied.

"Yo what the fuck is wrong with you? I ain't fucking nobody but you! I thought we already established this shit once before. Why you always think I am lying to you? You come over here every day to fuck so when do I have time to fuck other bitches, Rasheedah?" Bishop was loud and wide awake at this point.

"Bishop what the fuck ever! I am done with your lying ass," I said as I grabbed my purse and keys leaving Bishop in the bed, confused and upset.

I exited his house and hauled ass to my car and drove home.

Driving home with the radio off was never a good idea for my overanalytical ass. I hate that I have to be so cruel to Bishop when he is really that dude I can turn to. When I am in need, he is there. Whether it's for dick, for conversation, for weed, or even to whip a muthafucker's ass, Bishop is that dude I can always depend on.

127

I had felt terrible about how I treated Bishop but if I told him why I always opted to leave rather than have a sleepover, he would likely freak out and stop dealing with me altogether. Oh well, I'd make it my business to just drive over to his house tomorrow and give him some makeup sex and head.

I arrived home in five minutes. It was so late and pitch black outside that I was nervous to open my car door. I was so afraid to get out of my car that I sat still for over fifteen minutes before making a run for it. I didn't see anyone lurking but was always paranoid in the dark and oftentimes my anxiety would get the best of me. When I finally did get out of the car I held my purse as tight as I could and bolted from the driveway to the front door. I damn near broke the key trying to open the door. When I finally got inside I was panting and my heart was racing as if I'd just sprinted around the block.

"Thank you, Jesus!" I spoke in between breaths.

When I got inside the house I turned on all of the lights and shouted for my brother from the living room refusing to climb the stairs until he responded. The house was too quiet, and I was always afraid to go upstairs when no one else was home.

"Rahmel!" I shouted. When he did not answer I began to panic, "Rahmel! Rahmel, are you here?" I screamed at the top of my lungs repeatedly. Still no response. I screamed a few more times before I finally heard a voice.

"Yeah, what is it?" he finally groggily replied, startled and frustrated by my shouting.

"I am sorry, it's just that I was scared. When you didn't answer the first time, I thought you weren't home. I didn't

know if you stayed at a friend's house or not," I said as I climbed the stairs with confidence, feeling safe now. I smiled as I passed his room making my way towards the attic. He rolled his eyes as he shook his head with blatant annoyance.

"Rasheedah, you really need help. You are afraid of your own damn shadow," he said and then walked back into his room slamming the door. I deserved his attitude for waking him out of his sleep in the wee hours of the morning.

"Love you, brother. Goodnight, and again, I'm so sorry for waking you," I said. I was so relieved that he was home that I ran upstairs to my room, turned on the lights, and fell soundly asleep.

The next morning, I woke up excited that I'd slept through the night. It was the start of a great morning. I showered and headed downstairs to make breakfast.

Rahmel was already in the kitchen and he had company, some new girl he was seeing. At seventeen years old, Rahmel was young, wild, and carefree. He often had overnight company and my parents never seemed to mind, so today was nothing new.

"What up, what up, what up!" I cheerfully greeted them both.

"Good morning," the girl replied with a giggle and smile.

"Oh, someone's in a good mood. Good morning crazy girl," Rahmel teased grabbing my face and giving me a wet kiss on the cheek. Of my two brothers, Rahmel and I were the closest. He was four years younger than me, but we were the best of friends and got along great. Whenever he needed me, I was always there, and the same thing applies to me. At times, our camaraderie was tested by his reckless behavior but without hesitation, I was always willing to ride for him. In fact, that was the case when it came to both Raheem and our older brother, Rodney. Raheem was spoiled. Rodney and I protected him from a lot because he is the youngest and therefore considered the baby of the family.

Rahmel was making breakfast for him and his guest. Anytime, our parents were away, he took full advantage of the house, transitioning it into a full-fledge bachelor's pad.

"What are you making us for breakfast, emphasis on 'us'?" I said, inviting myself to eat breakfast with him and his friend.

"I'm about to make Belgian waffles, eggs, and sausage, right after I smoke some 'wake and bake'," he said with a cheerful smile.

"Cool, I'm right on time. Roll up," I said referring to the open invitation to smoke up my brother's marijuana.

We smoked some weed and enjoyed a lovely breakfast. Needless to say, there were no leftovers. After breakfast, I retired to the living room and watched some television while Rahmel and his friend went back up to his room. I began thinking of a way to smooth things over with Bishop. I liked Bishop more than I cared to admit. Yet, I constantly worried

that things with us would be short-term. When it came to relationships, all of mine were short-lived because I constantly run away. Even if I am interested in the person, I often find myself ending relationships sooner than they began to avoid the other person from ending things first. For as long as I can remember, I have had a phobia of someone leaving me before I could leave them. So, most of my relationships were not relationships at all, but mostly sexual encounters or flings.

I dialed Bishop expecting him to cuss me out for skipping out on him as I have done so many times before to avoid sleeping overnight. Typically, he would be upset with me for a couple of days, and then eventually we would kiss and make up.

"Hello," he said flatly.

"Good morning, rise and shine!" I said happily trying to break the ice.

Silence.

F.E.A.R. YOUR SANITY

"Uh, how are you doing?" I asked not knowing what to say.

"I'm busy," he spoke bluntly.

"Oh, I wanted to know if you wanted to…"

"Call me back later, I'm in the middle of something," he cut me off and hung up the phone.

I was crushed, it felt like it was over. Although Bishop and I did not connect on a deep level, I was hurt that our sexual escapades were over. After two years, he was finally done with me. I figured the day would come soon it was almost as if I was anticipating it to happen before it actually did. Over the years I had gotten accustomed to people leaving.

As hard as it was, I was relieved that Bishop had ended it. He was so sexy, so fine, and so popular, I really did not feel like I was good enough to keep him happy. I never spoke with him after that call.

*

A few months after it ended, my brother Rahmel called my cell while I was out of town to inform me of some disturbing news.

"Sheeda, where you at?" he asked as soon as I answered the phone.

"Well, hello to you too, you must be missing me already," I joked but he did not laugh which was unlike him.

"What's wrong, brother?" I asked bracing myself for bad news.

"It's Bishop, the guy you were dealing with from up the hill. I heard he got shot and killed tonight by a cop. Heard it was during an attempted robbery that had gone wrong," he said.

I could not believe what I was hearing. Despite our turbulent relationship, I was crushed to learn that Bishop had been killed. I never got a chance to say goodbye to him.

Rest In Peace Bishop

Hypocrisy

When I awoke, I was shivering cold, groggy, and disgusted with myself. I was disappointed in myself that yet again I had had another bad dream about what happened to me as a kid. It was so defeating that my experiences as a kid were still affecting my life in the present.

I got up from the cold wet bed slowly to prevent the wet clothes from touching my skin directly. It was already cold in the attic and wet clothes only made it worse. I removed every stitch of clothing and fought back tears reliving this same routine for countless days and nights for as long as I could remember.

Ashamed to run into anyone downstairs, I opted to clean myself from the urine stench by taking a birdbath from the bathroom sink up in the attic before heading downstairs to take an actual shower. I showered quickly. Ran back to my room to flip over my mattress for the umpteenth time, opened all of the windows for air to circulate the stench out and lit incense, and stuffed the comforter in the closet on top of the one from previous nights. I had my routine down to a science. Once the coast was clear, I'd load my comforters into my car's trunk and take a drive to the laundromat for washing. My paranoia wouldn't allow me to risk someone in the house finding out my secret, so I never washed my clothes or comforters at home, I always went to the laundromat.

As I walked down the stairs after having completed my routine, I could smell the sweet aroma of fried apples. Sweet cinnamon and sugared apples filled the air. I smile because I knew that it had to be Otis cooking in the kitchen as he religiously did every Sunday morning for the family. He was a firm believer in staying home and cooking rather than spending money and eating out which was my mother's preference.

Otis brought a certain calmness and sanity to our household that had never existed in our home. His southern values changed our family dynamics as they served as the blueprint to what a true family was supposed to be. What Otis shared made a huge difference in our lives from before my mother had met him.

"Good morning Otis!" I said. "When did y'all get back?" I greeted him by rubbing his back as he stood over the six-burner range of the state-of-the-art culinary kitchen he had built to compliment his reputable cooking talents.

"Hey, Gal! How's it going?" he asked as he prepared to make homemade waffles. Rahmel and I often attempted to replicate Otis's waffles, but never could we duplicate them.

"Everything's fine. Hey Ma," I spoke to my mother in between my conversation with Otis as he cooked.

"What's going on?" she replied flatly.

"Nothing," I flatly replied.

"So Otis, how's the family in Virginia?" I asked as I watched him prepare a complete breakfast as my mother sat and fiddled through Sunday's newspaper.

"Everybody's doing just fine Gal. They all asked about you all. You and your brothers," he said. Otis was listening to the radio, which is something that he enjoyed while cooking.

Every Sunday morning Otis and mother would listen to a Sunday radio panel that discussed African American issues called the Open Line. The Open Line was a nationally syndicated show that covered everything from political campaigns to police brutality and inner-city violence.

"What's the topic this morning, Otis?" I asked, ending our conversation and trying to tune in like him. It was my stepfather who introduced me to politics and becoming more socially aware of the injustices within the African American community.

"They're talking about the young girl who left her kids alone in the house, stepped out for however long, and while she was gone a fire broke out. Those poor children burned to death in the fire," he compassionately said.

"That woman ought to be shot for doing them kids that way," my mother commented.

"Well, it's a sad situation because supposedly she was working when it happened," Otis gave the woman the benefit of the doubt.

"Hell no, Otis! They were little babies. She should have at least.." Mother said as I quickly cut her off.

"She should have at least, what?!" I interjected with fury ready to blast her.

"Well, let me finish, Rasheedah," she said with frustration.

"She could have at least had a neighbor come to check on them babies once in a while," she said.

I angrily shook my head in disgust. "Oh so is that what you did all the days and nights you left us in that apartment alone? How could you part your lips to judge her? You have no room to judge anybody's parental skills? Is this a joke?" I tried to laugh to keep from exploding.

"What do you mean by that Rasheedah? I worked two, sometimes three jobs to provide for y'all. Y'all ain't never go without, so what are you talking about? my mother defensively replied.

"Ma, knock it off! You weren't always working. We'd be sitting in that apartment for days without seeing the sight of our mother or any adult for that matter! So, don't even make it seem like you were Mary frigging Poppins," I said.

"Well, Rasheedah, there is no handbook to raising children. If you ever decide to have children of your own, all that you can do is the best that you can," Otis said attempting to defuse the disagreement between his wife and me.

"Oh well, no worries there because she is too mean to allow anybody close enough to her to have kids. Out of all my kids, Rasheedah would be the last to have children, if she ever will," my mother said nonchalantly with a slight laugh.

I was so angry that sweat started to form on my forehead. I was boiling and wanted to defend myself from my mother's harsh and hypocritical words but I was trying my hardest not to be disrespectful towards her.

"Let me leave before I go off," I announced grabbing a piece of fruit from the fruit basket, heading for the door.

"Now Rasheedah, I'm cooking all of this food and now you are leaving?" Otis said with disappointment.

"I'm sorry Otis but I just cannot be bothered. It is too beautiful of a morning and I can't deal with it, I am not in the mood. If I stay, things will get ugly and I will once again be kicked out on the street, because that is what all good mothers do to their children," I sarcastically said.

"You can't deal with what, Rasheedah!? If you got something to say, then just say it! Ain't no skin off my ass, I don't care what your black ass think about me anyway!" my mother said looking at me, her eyes shooting into me as if they were darts. She rolled her eyes and pointed her manicured fingernail at me, revealing her 4-carat platinum wedding set, "bitch what you think of me has never mattered!"

"Same the fuck here!" I replied.

"Get the fuck out, right goddamn now!" Mother screamed.

"Sandra! You cannot keep doing this to that gal," Otis shouted.

"Otis, this bitch will not talk to me any kind of way as if she is the mother and I'm the goddamn child," Mother said.

"Oh so, you really believe in your heart that you are a good mother. Now that is the funniest shit under the sun," I laughed aloud obnoxiously as I walked out the front door and towards my car.

I Just Want to Be Loved

"You came all the way here just to see where I lived," he asked intensely staring at me as I sat across from him on the worn leather chair. "Come sit over here next to me," he slyly smiled revealing a deep dimple indented on the left side of his cheek.

Stephen was definitely my type. He was six foot three inches tall, light-skinned, with gorgeous slanted brown eyes, jet black hair, and thick black eyebrows with a full dark beard. The man was fine. I met him one evening at a bar with my hairstylist turned homegirl, Felicia, and another acquaintance of mine, her sister Raynell. Felicia was dating Stephen's cousin, Tone, and it was her who introduced me to Stephen. She informed me that he had recently relocated from North Carolina to New Jersey and was looking for a friend to show him around. We clicked and after the initial meet-up and began spending time together. Stephen and the others were seven years older than me, but we all connected well. Oftentimes, Felicia, Tone, Stephen, and I would get together a few times a month to barhop.

"You are so chocolate," he said.

"Don't say that. Is that all you see when you look at me? All you see is my dark-skinned complexion" I asked offensively.

"I didn't mean to insult you. I love your skin, chocolate is my favorite," he smiled widely making me forget that I never appreciated people referencing my deep hue. He was so attractive, so his admiration of my skin tone was well received.

"Oh, so if you like chocolate, how about I let you taste some," I flirted back removing my bikinis from under my skirt and throwing them at him. I so desperately wanted him to like me. "Would you enjoy that?" I asked.

He caught my bikinis and smelled them, "yummy. I surely would enjoy that and can show you better than I can tell you. Be back in a second," he said getting up from the sofa and leaving the living room. He walked in the back towards the bedroom. After what seemed like forever, I decided that he was taking too long and walked in the back, thinking that Stephen was in the bedroom straightening up. When I got there, the bedroom was empty, and Stephen was not on the double mattress that lay on the floor with no box spring or frame. Nowhere to be found, I headed towards the bathroom.

I opened the door and saw Stephen leaned over the sink. "Hey, do you want some of this chocolate or not? You just left me out there all alone," I said.

Unsettled that I had walked in on him, Stephen quickly covered the mirror that was placed atop the sink.

"Have some patience, I will be right with you," he said never turning to look at me.

"What are you doing in here?" I asked walking in front of the sink to see what he was hiding.

"I said I'll be right with you in a second babe, just relax and go back in the living room," he said motioning for me to leave the bathroom.

"No, I'm not leaving. What are you hiding, Stephen?" I asked lifting up his left arm that was protecting whatever he was attempting to hide from me.

"It's nothing, baby. Just a little coke. I want you so bad. Let me finish in here and I will show you some different type of lovemaking," he said confidently as he looked into my eyes and rubbed the nape of my neck. His eyes asserted the desire to give me pleasure. He was so fucking fine. I wanted him just as much as he wanted me but then I began to overthink in my mind if his intentions were genuine.

"Oh, so you need to use coke to make love to me," I questioned suspiciously as I assumed that he needed to take drugs because he did not find me attractive enough to have sex with.

"Baby not at all! Would you stop thinking like that? Please stop thinking negatively. You are thinking that I don't want you but look at this," he said turning to face me and revealing an apparent erect penis through his joggers. "This makes me feel like superman all night long baby. I want to please you in every way for as long as you want me to. You are about to see what's up," he said picking up a shortened straw from the mirror and then bending down. Stephen snorted one of the lines from the mirror making all the white powder

142

disappear. He rose his head quickly, revealing a slightly reddened nose that appeared inflamed. His eyes jolted as he pinched his nose. "Uh-oh, baby I'm about to fuck you so good! You are about to get it. You about to get all this country Carolina dick!" he warned as he pinched my ass cheek. "You about to get this dick, you are going to get it!" he chanted as he clapped his hands and laughed aloud.

I had never seen anyone use coke before. His excitement to fuck me made me feel so desirable. "You want this chocolate pussy, how bad do you want it" I teased as I began kissing his neck and rubbing his broad stocky shoulders.

"Oh my fucking God I'm gonna fuck the shit out of you," he said as he began to tongue-kiss me. "You're all I want, let me have you," he said urgently. I was baffled at how passionate the drug had made him. He desired me so badly and it made me curious if the drug would make me just as passionate as he.

"You want me to fuck you all night? Would that make you feel good?" I attempted to sound as confident in my sexual abilities as he was.

"Oh hell yeah baby, fuck me all night muthafucking long! I want you so bad oh my fucking God, I got to have you" he shouted lifting up my skirt. "Let me taste your pussy," he said getting on his knees. His anxiousness took me to a level of zeal that I had never experienced. This man was fine as shit and he wanted me so bad that he was begging to taste me. His fondness for me made me feel worthy to be with him. Drugs or not, he wanted me and only me. I felt vindicated from feeling unpretty and not good enough after Bishop abruptly ended our relationship. Stephen redeemed my brokenness with his yearn for me.

I kneeled down and speedily snorted the remaining line of powder. It shocked both of us.

"Ooooooo shit!! My baby about that muthafucking life!" he cheered. "Oh my God, where the fuck have you been all my life! My baby hit that shit like a champ!" he exhilarated as he began to flick his tongue.

The effects of the drug were immediate and so intense that I nearly collapsed. It began to overtake my five-foot one-inch petite frame instantaneously. My nose burned and my head felt heavy but then there was a swift forceful rush and feeling of elation that swallowed me whole. The feeling of love drowned the entire bathroom. It struck us both. Stephen cried out, "I love you, baby. You are the love of my life. I fucking crave you. Let me stick my dick inside of you. Oh God let me make you feel so good, baby," he whined.

At that moment, I felt joyful, beautiful, and in love. I hopped on top of the sink, slid Stephen's joggers and briefs down, and guided him into me. I had only known Stephen for about three weeks, but it felt right. My consequential act of impulse seemed to turn him on even more, "I'm coming, I'm coming, I'm coming! Damn baby look at how you got me," he screamed as he exploded inside of me.

F.E.A.R. YOUR SANITY

Cocaine

Bumps in the car, midnight horrors reign
Caine to numb the pain
Come the fuck down
Same troubles
same heartache
Shit remains the same
Staying up
I no longer give a fuck
From day one
Life for me sucked
Shit been fucked up
No mother, no father, no love
Been down on my luck
No one ever cared
Perverts hurt me
Nobody was ever there
So with me they had their way
Crash and burn
Troubles here to stay
Unworthy, dark skin, no trophy
Want someone to choose me
Muthafuckers disappear from my life
Always leaving
When they do, it's open season
They always go away
Get faded
Feel the love
Thru euphoric pleasure
Is where I want to stay
Less pressure
And the sex be on a whole other level
Fuck me so good
Make me feel special

I Don't Know

"How did it end?" he asked.

"What?" I replied sounding startled as I tried to comprehend the question. Isaiah had a way of digging deep into spaces and places that I either was not ready to go or was too ashamed to go.

"Has your drug abuse ceased or are you still battling addiction?" he asked matter-of-factly.

"Well, I may smoke a little weed every now and again to relax me," I admitted.

"What about your use of cocaine, alcohol, and prescription drugs?" he interjected.

"No, I gave all of that up after I became a mother," I replied. "I mean I drink socially but I no longer drink to get drunk."

"Did you seek treatment for any of the substance abuse?" he asked.

"No!" I sharply projected my voice. I was starting to grow impatient with Isaiah's line of questioning. All at once, the discussion seemed to go from a conversation to interrogation. I was beginning to feel that he was judging my poor decisions and choices.

"Rasheedah, I do not mean to probe. It is not my intention to offend. However, I need to understand if you are still battling addiction. It is the only way that I can help you, which is your reasoning for being here," Isaiah said.

"Isaiah, the answer is no, I no longer use any type of hard drugs. As for alcohol, yes, I do drink socially. Once in a while, I may smoke marijuana but even that has not happened in years. I only do that on occasions. I have always been afraid to get addicted to drugs. The reason being is that I saw what addiction did to one of my favorite people. Also because one night I was so high that I think I was date raped by someone I trusted," I said staring at Isaiah to see if he would react to my irresponsibility.

"Well, I applaud that you were able to desist from those destructive habits. You are a strong woman, Rasheedah. Not everyone can kick bad habits, especially as it relates to addiction. You mentioned that you may have been date raped. Do you care to elaborate on that? Talk to me about when this happened and the details of how it potentially occurred," he said.

"It happened during the time I had begun dating Kyle's father, Stephen. I may have been nineteen or maybe even twenty. Years prior, I used to work at Walgreens, it was my first job. I met a guy there named Derrick, he was older than me. At that time I was 16-years-old and he was 21-years-old. He was a chill guy, very handsome, and admired by all of the girls at the job. I remember him being so nice to me because he was friends with a few of my cousins, they all graduated from the same high school. So, I trusted Derrick because I considered him a friend of my family.

Fast forward, years later I ran into him at my then job at Bloomingdales. He gave me his number and offered for us to hang out sometimes. Not thinking anything of it, I was up to hang out with him because he was still a cool guy and very good-looking. We ended up hanging out that same weekend and I recall him picking me up from my mother and stepdad's house. He came in and spoke to the family like the gentle giant that I thought he was. Derrick was well over six feet five inches tall and was a laid-back kind of guy. Although laid-back, he was the social guy that everyone enjoyed hanging out with because he was a lot of fun to be around.

At this time, I was already involved with Stephen and had already begun experimenting with party drugs. I can admit that I did do a line of coke before leaving my parent's house. It was because I wanted to seem cool around Derrick since I had not seen him in years. Also, I did not want to overthink him having invited me out. Based on his dating history of girls he dealt with, I was not his type. Derrick was into Asian and Latina girls.

Anyway, I had left my car parked and hopped into Derrick's Expedition. We went to a bar far out on Route 46, which was nowhere near the area we lived. The place was about thirty minutes from my parent's place in Fairfield somewhere. He told me he wanted to introduce me to some of his friends and I was fine with that. We met up with a group of his friends and their girlfriends at the bar. I was so high and turned up that I really did not need any alcohol since I was already rambunctious and my alter-ego had been activated by the lines, but Derrick kept buying me drinks. I could not finish one drink before he was bringing me another. I recall sitting at the bar and out of nowhere him kissing me on my lips and that was it. Everything else about that night was and still is one big blur. The next morning, I awoke in Derrick's bed completely nude laying in piss and smelling of vomit. I asked him what had happened and why was I naked?"

"And what did he say?" asked Isaiah.

"He asked me what about last night did I remember? Strangely, I could not remember anything, with the exception of what I just told you. And that was weird because I had a very high tolerance when it came to alcohol. After all, I started drinking around twelve or thirteen. I cannot recall a time where I had completely blanked out and didn't remember anything," I said.

"Why do you suspect that you were sexually assaulted?" he asked.

"Because Derrick was also nude in bed and, his dick, I mean his penis had dried up semen on it. And there was dried semen in my pubic hair," I said.

"I asked him did we have sex but he insisted that we had not. Then Derrick kept letting me know that he loved my matching bra and panty set," I shrugged.

"I don't understand. He said he liked your panties?" Isaiah sounded confused.

"Yes, but he said it several times. He said "nice panties by the way. They are very sexy,"" I replied.

"And then what happened?" Isaiah asked.

"He suggested that I take a shower because I had urinated and vomited. There was some vomit in my hair as well as on the sheets. I said no but he kept on insisting. Something seemed off and I did not feel right about the entire situation, so I asked him to just take me home, and he did," I said.

"Had you ever gotten that intoxicated before where you would urinate and vomit all over yourself," Isaiah asked?

"Yes, especially when I wanted to appear normal and break out of my recluse shell. Being high or drunk, or both always gave me confidence. It made me become the life of any party. The feeling was like putting on a jacket of your favorite alter-ego who happened to have superpowers. When I was high, I was social, my self-confidence was heightened and I also stayed out of my head, meaning I never overanalyzed anything. With that said though, I always remember what happened the night before. So, it was odd not remembering anything," I said.

"Yes, but I am concerned about the guy's standoffish conduct. Was his behavior strange during the drive back to your parent's house?" Isaiah asked.

"The drive was mostly quiet. Yes, Derrick's behavior was strange, he did not seem like himself at all. Once he dropped me off, I never heard from him again. In fact, he never called me again and I never physically seen him anywhere after that," I concluded.

"It certainly sounds like something out of the ordinary did happen. I mean, you know your body and the mere fact that he was also nude does seem suspect. Did you ever go to the hospital to get checked out or report the incident to the police?" Isaiah asked.

"No, I did not. Deep down a part of me feels strongly that Derrick did something to me. Every drink I had that night was handed to me by him. Perhaps he did put something into one of the drinks, I don't know. There is something that I feel he was keeping from me. But I also blame myself for being so high and getting so drunk. Maybe he did not put anything in my drink, maybe that was the one time that I was so intoxicated that I blanked out and forgot what happened," I said.

"Rasheedah, that could be the case but at no point should Derrick have been naked with semen coming from his penis. It is unfortunate but it sounds like maybe he did violate you and you were so out of it that you have no memory of it.

152

Shifting gears, who was the person in your life that got hooked on drugs?" he asked.

"It was my uncle, my mother's brother. Growing up, I admired him. He was everything to me! He even brought me my first pair of clog shoes, they were so beautiful! You couldn't tell me anything!" I laughed as I reflected on one of my favorite pastimes with my uncle Richard.

"He was the first man that I had ever loved but he also was the first to break my heart. Uncle Richard had always had his own apartment and it was always decked out. My brothers and I enjoyed spending time with him over at his place because he would take us places and play with us. He was always so much fun and for me he made me feel safe. One day things with him began to change. Uncle Richard had no place to live, so Mother let him come to live with us. From that point, his addiction progressed rapidly. When he was at the house, he was no longer fun but very irritable, disinterested, or spaced out. In my late teens, I started to see the horrors of his addiction. There were times that he would go missing for long extended periods. Mother ended up telling us that he was battling drugs. When I found out that he started off using cocaine and later had gotten strung out on crack two things happened: number one, my love for him changed and number two, I immediately stopped my sporadic cocaine use. Seeing him deteriorate scared me out of ever doing another bump or line of coke. And it forever changed our connection. It changed so much that even now today, I do not have a relationship with him.

"Why don't you two have a relationship? Is your uncle still addicted to drugs?" Isaiah asked.

"No. I mean, I don't know since I haven't seen my uncle in years. As I said, my view of him changed when he was living at the house. Things had gotten so bad that he began stealing from my stepdad. He would steal things all the time and it divided the household. One time he stole my stepdad's car and sold it for drugs. Mother never kicked him out, no matter what he would do. After a while, I began to hate him for all that he had put the family through. At one point he was my superhero and then he turned into a crackhead," I said.

"Rasheedah, addiction is a disease that is extremely difficult to overcome. Sadly, many people never can kick the habit. Imagine if you had gotten strung out from your experimental drug use, would your outlook change?" Isaiah asked.

"I don't know," I shrugged. "As I said, I stopped using it in my early twenties. Yes, I had done it a few times, but I was never addicted to it. I did not like the way coke made me feel and only used it for its heightened social and sexual gratification abilities. I was already an anxious person but being on coke made me even more paranoid. So, I only used it for that specific purpose," I said.

F.E.A.R. YOUR SANITY

"It is something to consider, what if you had gotten addicted? You have said that you used drugs to escape traumatic life events, correct? Have you ever considered that perhaps your uncle took drugs to self-medicate and rid himself of his own trauma? Drug addiction is not easy on the family. It often leaves incurably deep wounds, similar to you permanently severing ties with someone you once deemed to be one of your favorite people. Well, I would encourage you to have compassion. Have compassion for not only your uncle but for anyone struggling with addiction. Also, count your blessings that you were able to escape getting addicted. But soften your heart, ease your stance a bit, because everyone struggles with something. While your vice may not be drug abuse, you admit to struggling with other things. Furthermore, you hate to be judged by others. I encourage you to reconnect with your uncle. Give it some thought," Isaiah said.

"At some point, I would like to cover generational trauma. Maybe we can even identify some potential examples within your own family and how it impacts how you relate to others. Just from what you have shared, I am interested if there are potential generational patterns to explore," Isaiah warmly continued. "How does that sound?"

I could not answer Isaiah because my heart felt so heavy. I had been so angry with my uncle and in the past had gone so far as to verbally attack him by calling him "weak", "a loser" or even the dreadful word "crackhead." I was overwhelmed with what I had done to someone I genuinely loved.

"Isaiah, I would like to close tonight's session with a poem I had written years ago while in high school called Euphoria, Bad Habits," I said wiping the tears flowing down my face.

"Of course. Take it away," Isaiah said.

F.E.A.R. YOUR SANITY

Euphoria Bad Habits

This shit ain't right
Euphoria, bad habits
Anger spells and sleepless nights
Worried if I'd ever see you again or
if this last fix would remove you from my life

No! No, no don't go! You have to be here to see me grow
Flashbacks to sober times when you were the highlight of my life
I wasn't around you often but your spirit always was a reassurance
that everything was gonna be alright

You would take us to Liberty State Park, you remember you brought
my first pair of clogs?
Oh God please don't take him away from us
Lord why? Does my cries matter to you at all?
As a child I just couldn't understand
Leave, stay, leave, comeback,
this made no sense, God I need my uncle back!

Growing older and witnessing the battle of addiction, forced me into
a different position
Outrage! Anger! Hurt and disdain
I forced myself to hate you, just so I didn't have to deal with the pain
I would be able to sleep at night, rather than to wait to hear the front
door squeal open and you stumble into the house in the wee hours of
the night

I don't have to ponder if you are dead or alive,
don't have to accept you coming home after two-month binges
weighing ninety pounds soaking wet
Your physical appearance taking me and everyone else by total
surprise

I forced myself to hate you and disassociate all love for you out of
anger, constant nightmares wondering if you were hurt or in danger
My heart was always heavy and I always cared
I just hated that you allowed addiction to take control, I missed you
so much, Life just never seemed to be fair

F.E.A.R. YOUR SANITY

When you were gone I would go into the basement and beg God that
you would come home, I would beg and cry for you to God until I
dozed off to sleep

Days, weeks, months later you would show up, but I resented you for
being so weak

I resented you for being selfish, I resented you for being helpless
Until one day it dawned on me, we all fall short of God's glory
As an adult I battle my own addictions, and it puts your situation into
perspective, We are all works in progress, I had no right to be
subjective

I was a child and its hard to accept change, its hard when life as you
know it is no longer the same

All that I can say now is that I could never be against you
My love is stronger than your addiction and far more powerful
I love and miss my uncle so much, I regret ever treating him wrong
Isaiah, thank you for showing me a different outlook,
which is why I had to revise the words to this poem

Codependence

It did not take long after meeting Stephen for me to realize that he was not the one for me. Although he was physically attractive, with a great personality he had nothing else going for himself. Just a few months into dating him, I learned that Stephen was an opportunist looking for a come-up. When we met, he was sleeping on his cousin's couch in a one-bedroom apartment and his intentions were fixated on improving his overall circumstances. He did not have much and needed help. I had never had a long-term monogamous commitment with anyone. Stephen was available and showed interest so, I had dived headfirst, despite knowing that it was a beautiful lie.

At the time I was a full-time sophomore in college pursuing an undergraduate degree in sociology. So, during the day I was in class, and in the evenings and weekends, I worked at Bloomingdales. Typically, I would spend the remainder of my time with friends but once Stephen was in the picture, I had no time for anyone else. He had no job, no transportation, no money, and no other prospects in the picture. Therefore, Stephen found refuge in me. He clung to me so tightly that I hardly ever had any time for myself outside of school, work, and him.

Each day after my classes ended Stephen would have already inundated my inbox with dozens of text messages filled with words of affirmation. "Thinking of you baby, you are my world. Please stop by the apartment when your classes are over. I miss you so much baby please call me, I am over here lovesick," he would often say.

The truth is, Stephen was broke, bored, and alone. Like clockwork every single time I was on my way to see him, I'd receive a call from him. He would say, "baby I'm hungry, can you buy me something to eat; baby, can you stop by the liquor store and buy me a twelve-pack of Coors and some cigarettes; baby, I want to fuck you long and hard tonight, can you cop us some blow and trees; or baby, what time are you coming, I am lonely and need you." It was always something that Stephen needed that he expected me to supply. It did feel good to be needed and wanted by someone so fine. After a while, it got to a point where he no longer had to call with requests. I would call him every day after school or work and ask him what he needed before I made my way over there.

He depended on me to meet all his needs. I obliged his requests because in return Stephen immersed himself into professing his love for me. He filled my love tank abundantly by claiming me as his lady and by showering me with compliments. Every time I would take him to dinner or to a movie someplace, Stephen would go above and beyond to proclaim his adoration of me. He expected all my time and hated for me to be away from him. Whenever I was, he would text me nonstop until I reunited with him. My time was no longer mine; he absorbed my space as if we were one. He even told people that I was his wife because I was the best he had ever had.

I soaked up the endearing sentiments like a sponge even though I was cognizant that he was embellishing his feelings for me. The attention he gave me was intoxicating and so addictive, I did all that I could to keep him happy. When he wanted to party, we partied hard with my money. When he wanted to go places, I would drive him or let him drive my car and pay for the gas. When he wanted to fuck all night, it was my money buying the coke. When he wanted to get wasted, it was my money used to cop the weed, pills, and booze that we indulged in. When he needed clothes, haircuts, time away from his cousin's apartment, it was my money that provided whatever he needed. I treated him like a king because he chose me when I'd never been chosen before by anyone on a long-term basis. Things with us seemed to be going great but one day it all changed.

Breakthrough

Three years into our relationship I had made it to my senior year in college and had begun working for the State of New Jersey in the judiciary sector. I even helped Stephen get a full-time job as a machinist at a manufacturing plant. We each were making a decent living and decided to get an apartment together. Things were going well. We were functional addicts but worked hard to sustain food, shelter, and whatever vices we indulged in. Those vices included alcohol, weed, pills, and coke. It was not an everyday occurrence, but we were known to throw house parties every weekend and would often wallow in a drunken stupor with friends. This behavior went on until one day I had gotten so sick that I could not stop vomiting.

It was not unusual for me to excrete or defecate if I had consumed too much alcohol from the night before, but this feeling was different from the typical purging from alcohol. I went to the emergency room with a complaint of flu-like symptoms but soon learned that the prognosis was much more serious.

"When was your last menstrual period?" the male nurse asked.

"I don't know. My periods are irregular, so I never keep up with the dates," I responded.

"Well, I'll need a urine sample from you. The bathroom is right this way Miss…" He spoke but I quickly cut him off and declined to give a urine sample.

"Actually, I peed before I got here and don't have to go right now," I lied. The truth is I was afraid that the urine result would reveal my drug use. I never gave my urine even when I went for the drug screening with the State of New Jersey. I used someone else's urine. Stephen had taught me how to pass a drug test and it worked. I used the urine of an acquaintance who did not use any drugs. She peed into an empty small plastic medicine bottle and sealed it with its lid. I went for the screening with the bottle lodged in between my breasts. When I poured the urine into the cup, it was still warm from my body temperature. I never got caught and was hired for the job.

Thankfully, the nurse did not pick up on my reluctance, so he did not push the issue, "No worries. The doctor will be in soon to perform an examination."

"Thank you," I smiled.

When the doctor arrived, she performed the examination. She began with checking my breathing, ears, nose, and throat. She then asked that I lay back on the table and began pressing on my belly. She abruptly stopped, "Miss Taylor, when was your last period, again?" she inquired.

"Uh, I am not sure. My periods are irregular and have been for quite some time," I replied.

"Yeah, but how long ago do you think it's been? Two months, three months?" she probed.

"Umm, maybe around that," I guessed pleased with her approximation.

"Did the nurse get a urine sample from you?" she asked.

"No," I answered flatly.

"Miss Taylor, we need a urine sample," she advised.

"For what?" I asked as I grew irritated.

"Your uterus seems awfully high, it seems to be elevated to here," she said pressing around my belly button.

"Okay, and what does that mean?" I asked as I began to lose my patience.

"Miss Taylor, I think that you're pregnant. Certainly, feels that way. Please go to the bathroom and provide us with a urine sample to confirm the pregnancy."

My heart dropped to my stomach.

The drive home was unlike anything I had ever experienced. I felt overwhelmed by the news and had mixed emotions. Not only was I pregnant but I was sixteen weeks, which translated to four months. When the doctor tested my urine and confirmed what she'd expected, I could not believe what I was hearing.

"Are you fucking serious?" I asked not finding the presumed joke funny at all.

"No, this is not a joke. Ma'am, you are pregnant and pretty far along in your pregnancy. Additional testing is needed. I am sending you upstairs for bloodwork and an ultrasound," she said.

When I got onto the elevator to go upstairs for the added testing, I did something that I hardly have ever done since a little girl. I prayed repeatedly to myself, "God please let my baby be unharmed, please don't let my habits cause it any problems. Keep it from danger. If you allow my baby to be safe, I will change my whole life for good." When I left that hospital, I was a changed person. I had a life growing inside of me that I was now responsible for and protecting it was my only priority.

Prayer

God can you hear me, please accept my plea

I need you

For this is something I must do

It is for the betterment of my well being

And the little miracle I am carrying too

So please God I am asking you to see me through

I am determined to do well

I will listen to my body and learn self-discipline

Never have I tried to stop

Didn't realize my consumptions was considered an addiction

I got caught up trying to be accepted and noticed

Please guide me forward keep me strong and focused

It's helped me to silence demons that has haunted me for years

When no one cared it was these same addictions that help me

temporarily conquer my fears

Please grant me the perseverance to stay on track

It is only through you that all things are possible

Grant me the courage and restraint to permanently put down the

bottle

Breakdown

The pregnancy caused a major shift in my relationship with Stephen, who did not take the news well at all.

"Pregnant?" he responded with a look of shock. "You cannot be serious," he said.

"This is unbelievable, right? Surprising but yes, it is true though, I am having a baby," I said still shocked by the news myself.

"Dammit Rasheeda, what are you going to do? I don't know if I'm ready for a baby," he said.

I looked at him with hurtful teary eyes, "well, get ready Stephen because this baby didn't ask to come here. How can you even say something like that?" I asked as I wiped the tears away. Stephen ran over to hug me as I sat at our kitchen table.

"Babe, I didn't mean it like that. All I'm saying is that a baby will change everything," he pouted.

"Well, we'll just have to embrace the changes as they come. Everything will be okay," I said getting up off of the chair and walking into the bedroom to process his reaction to the pregnancy announcement. While he was upset that a baby was coming, he did nothing to prevent it from happening. From the very first time, Stephen and I never used condoms. Granted, the first time we had sex we both were high and being careless. Still even after that, we never practiced safe sex. The one time I suggested that we do, Stephen was adamant that he did not like the feeling of condoms. So, I never mentioned it to him again.

When I stopped partying, life was different. I was cautious and intentional about what I allowed around me or inside of me. I kept my promise and never engaged in the use of any harmful substances or alcohol from the moment I knew about the child that I was carrying. Undertaking a new lifestyle change caused a divisive relationship between Stephen and me. We would argue often, and he would accuse me of "not caring about anything but that goddamn baby."

Stephen's indulgence in drugs and alcohol worsened as I advanced further along in the pregnancy. The arguments grew more volatile, and a few times turned physical. When I was eight months pregnant, he had gotten so high and drunk that he began accusing me of being sexually active with someone else.

"Who the fuck baby is that?" he yelled. "We been fucking for three years, and you never got pregnant. Suddenly, you turn up pregnant. So, who is the goddamn daddy? Answer me bitch?" he screamed even louder. Scared that he would push me down as he had done weeks prior, I sat on the sofa silent watching Jamie Foxx portray Ray Charles in the movie Ray, refusing to join in Stephen's drug-induced tantrum.

"Oh, so you want to ignore me bitch, I will show your black ass that I ain't to be played with," he darted towards the door that led to our terrace. He went on to the terrace and returned with a can of lighter fluid that we used to fire up our grill when we would entertain friends. We had not invited anyone over in a while since I became pregnant. I refused to continue having those gatherings because all we ever seemed to do was get loud and wasted.

"You fucking bitch, who baby is that?" Stephen yelled as he doused the blanket that was wrapped around me with lighter fluid. "Who fucking baby is that?!" he continued to shout.

I frantically tried to get up from the couch but he kept pushing me back down, "Have a muthafucking seat! Tell me who you been with before I set this muthafucking place up in flames," he threatened.

"Baby I swear to God I haven't been with anyone else. This baby is yours Stephen! When would I have time to cheat on you? I swear to God baby, I would not do that to you! I would never even want to" I cried trying to convince him of my sincerity.

"You fucking lying ass bitch! You always claim to be at school or work, but you been out fucking around on me bitch and now you gonna die today!" he darted towards the kitchen. "Just let me get some matches," he said.

Without thought, I quickly unwrapped myself from the damp blanket and bolted down the steps and out the front door.

Once outside, I screamed for help and several neighbors emerged from their homes. Not realizing that I had no shoes, socks, or any appropriate clothes on, I hurried over to the couple that lived downstairs from us. I was braless and only wearing a drenched nightgown that clearly revealed my large belly.

"Help me please! Help me!" I pleaded. Our next-door neighbor brought out a blanket and draped it over my shoulders as he used his cell phone to call the police. "Mami, you no deserve this, Mami. You need to leave that man before he kills you. You good woman, no deserve this," he spoke in a strong Spanish accent. "Police coming. No worry Mami, I stay out here with you," he said consoling me as his wife joined us.

"Oh my God, I so sorry for you Mami. Come here," she said as she embraced me close into her bosom. I cried hysterically until the police arrived and placed Stephen under arrest for terroristic threats.

A month later, I gave birth to a baby boy. Up until going to the emergency room, I had been taking daily multivitamins but had no prenatal care and I also was engaging in weekly drinking and drugging behaviors, all of which could have caused the significant negative impact, but God answered my prayers. My son was born at six pounds, four ounces, and was deemed healthy. I was elated that he was unaffected by my irresponsibility. When I looked into his eyes for the first time, it was love at first sight. All this time what I thought was love was not love at all but infatuation. Cradling my son in my arms was the purest form of love and the only thing that consumed my mind were thoughts of gratitude.

"Thank you, Jesus! Hallelujah, thank you for hearing me. Thank you for answering my prayers God," I yelled startling my son, whom I named Kyle Jordan. Our cries filled the room, and for sure mine were tears of joy.

F.E.A.R. YOUR SANITY

My First Love

Your presence in my life forced me to change my previous ways

to become the woman that I am today, Your Mommy

No one else has ever meant the universe to me

Your happiness, your safety, your smile are Mommy's priorities

I love you more than life itself, simply there is no me without you

You are the best gift I am blessed to have, even if its without your

dad

Kyle, I am very glad to have you

No one else has made me re-evaluate my life and the people in it

Sifting through so-called friends and even family

Was necessary for this motherhood commitment

You are my responsibility

And stability, love and consistency is all that matters to me

Zero hesitation in eliminating my partying

God blessed me to be your Mom and you didn't ask to be here

Come hell or high water, I will always be there

No one can ever come in between you and me

The title of 'Mom' requires integrity

No matter what happens in this life

You are my son and will always mean the world to me

Rebirth

The birth of Kyle forced me to grow up. From the moment I laid eyes on him, my perspective on life and God completely changed. I now felt a sense of purpose and strived to better myself by doubling up on classes to ensure that I graduated on time with my graduating class, which was only six months away. With me working and going to school full-time, I solicited Stephen's support. I would need him to step up to the plate by taking care of Kyle in the evenings after work while I focused on completing my courses. He agreed and promised to do whatever it would take to keep his family intact.

Although it was only a few short months, I was exhausted at how hectic my schedule had become. Being away from my baby was difficult and I often would leave classes early or skip a class now and again to get home to Kyle before his bedtime.

One evening I arrived at our apartment earlier than Stephen expected. Before I could even open the door, I could hear Kyle crying. As a new mother, I had already gotten familiar with the different types of baby cries. On this evening, it was not a normal cry but seemed more like a wail of rage. I struggled to try to unlock the door as fast as I could to get upstairs to my baby. When I climbed all twenty-three steps, I found Kyle sitting in his swing alone bawling as SpongeBob

SquarePants played on the television screen. The television was so loud that it was apparent that the volume had been purposefully increased to drown out Kyle's cries. I picked him up and began rocking him back and forth. "It's alright, honey. Mommy is here. Alright, little man, Mommy is here," I said trying to relax him. While he did begin to calm down, he still seemed to be uncomfortable. I wiped his tears and kissed his cheek and noticed an unpleasant smell on Kyle's breath. I walked over to the swing to retrieve Kyle's baby bottle and was mortified at what I saw. Tears of fire and fury filled my eyes when I picked up the bottle and saw an amber-colored liquid that reeked of a sour beer odor.

"Muthafucker!" I screamed heading for the bedroom. Stephen was in the bed asleep when I stormed into the bedroom and jumped onto his back. "Muthafucker! Are you stupid, are you that fucking dumb!" I screamed as I clawed him.

"What's wrong?!" Stephen awoke surprised to see me. "I am sorry babe, I fell asleep. I worked so hard today at work," he slurred making it evident that he was intoxicated.

I continued to go insane. "You gave my baby beer, you sick son of a bitch! You are trying to kill my baby, you sick bastard! You are crazy," I exclaimed as I continued trying to kick his ass, beating on his back as if it were a drum. Stephen flung me onto the floor as the punches and kicks persisted.

"What the fuck are you talking about? I ain't trying to hurt my son! That's just crazy for you to even think some sick shit like that! A little beer won't kill him. My mama and daddy always used to put beer in my bottle. That helps babies sleep better. It worked for me like a charm," he hollered wiping blood from his scratched neck.

"That's exactly why you turned out the way you did! A broke ass loser! A druggie and drunk that ain't got shit and never will have shit! A country-ass piece of shit! Both of them set you up for failure!" I shouted as I stood up to go back into the living room where I could now hear Kyle screaming at the top of his lungs.

"What the fuck did you just say to me?" he stood to his feet to confront me. "What did you say to me you black ugly ass bitch!" he said grabbing me by the back of my hair. "I don't even like your black ass like that no more! You're boring as fuck, and since you had that baby you are fat and ugly as fuck! I don't even like fucking your fat ass anymore! Why do you think I don't even ask you for pussy? I don't want that fat shit! I'd rather go out and fuck other bitches! At least they can make my dick get hard! You are a turnoff now, you pasta-eating bitch! No fun having ass," he continued.

"Well, I have no use for your coked-up ass anyway, you have nothing to offer me. You never had anything to offer except some doped-up dick! Oh yes, and some compliments to fill my ears up so that you could continue to get what you wanted from me! You are a lame-ass user that I was already planning to get rid of!" I yelled.

"Oh really, I am only good for passing out dick, huh? Ask your mother how good my dick is. That's right ask her how she loves to make my dick hard. She is great at what she does," he laughed devilishly. "Don't look so surprised you, fat sloppy bitch! You just don't know, I could've crushed your little feelings a long time ago but she begged me not to tell," Stephen laughed hysterically. "Now you got the nerve to think you are better than somebody because you are about to graduate. So what bitch, you still fat! That is why your own mama can't stand you. I have heard her say time and time again that she hates your fucking guts. I am the best thing that ever happened to your monkey ass now you think you are too good for me. You don't need me now that you are getting your fancy degree, huh," he said swiftly turning and placing me in a headlock. His grip was so tight, I struggled to breathe as I fought to break free. I could not believe what I had just heard. I wanted to disintegrate, but all that I could think of was my son.

"Let me go! Let me go you sorry piece of shit! You are a sorry excuse of a man," I screamed tirelessly. "You are not even worth the sofa you used to sleep on at your cousin's dirty ass mice-infested ass house. I upgraded your lowlife ass, you are pathetic," I exclaimed continuing to degrade him.

I wiggled out of the headlock and Stephen yanked me by my hair. He tightened his grip on my shoulder-length hair and began to headbutt me across my face. The forceful thrust of his head plummeted against my nose causing it to bleed. He did it a second time and split my bottom lip open causing it to bleed before releasing me from his grasp.

"Who's the piece of shit, now? Who were you threatening to leave bitch?" he asked as his face glowed with anger.

"I said what the fuck I said!" I shouted as loud as I could.

Stephen began hitting me in my face with a closed fist landing punches to my eyes, nose, and temples. Repeatedly he continued to target my face with repetitive blows. I ran out of the bedroom into the hallway trying to get away, but he followed closely behind.

"Oh no! Bring your black ass back here! You want to talk shit like your ugly ass is better than me, I am about to do what I been wanting to do since you fucked my life up with a baby I never wanted! I already got four fucking sons in North Carolina, I never fucking wanted any more kids! You ruined my life up here in Jersey by pinning that baby on me," he exclaimed chasing me into the kitchen.

In an attempt to slow him down, I grabbed the first thing to prevent him from hitting me again, a George Foreman grill sitting on the kitchen counter. I threw it and hit him in the head, but he kept coming at me. Dazed from the headbutt and punches he'd thrown, I opened the drawers in the kitchen trying my best to find a weapon to defend myself. I picked up a seven-inch cleaver knife that was given to us as a housewarming gift. Ensuring that I had secured my grip of its handle, I quickly turned around to confront him. Unphased, Stephen went to grab the knife away from me but missed. He tried again a second time but this time when he came nearer to me, closing in the gap between us I flung the sharp end of the knife as fast as I could. It landed into Stephen's shoulder and neck area. The cleaver struck Stephen's clavicle bone causing him to shriek in pain.

"Ouch!!" he squealed and twitched as blood leaked everywhere.

"Bitch done cut me! The bitch done cut me! Oh shit, you really cut me! You muthafucking cut me! Oh God," he bellowed in pain.

I ran into the living room and picked Kyle up, grabbed his coat, a diaper bag, and immediately left. We got to my best friend Lorraine's house in a matter of ten minutes, a trip that would typically take over fifteen minutes on ordinary days.

*

"Rasheeda, he could have killed you and Kyle. You need to finally be done with him. You have Kyle to think about," she pleaded with tears streaming down her face. She held Kyle in her arms, who had returned to his beamingly cheerful and active self. "I love y'all and don't want to see this end badly. If he's not going to clean up his life, you have to move on with yours," said Lorraine.

"It is finally over. Today Stephen showed me the real him. All this time I was sleeping with a man who apparently was fucking my mother. Can you believe that? I was confiding and being vulnerable with a man telling him all about the hurt behind my mother resenting me and how dysfunctional our relationship has always been, only for the man who I thought loved me to turn around and use my vulnerabilities against me and do the unthinkable. And thought it was funny. To him he thought it was funny and was laughing the whole time he spoke about it" I quivered as I spoke the horrid words, crying even harder as they left my lips.

"Oh my God, Sheedah, I am so sorry," Lorraine held me tightly with one arm while she held Kyle with the other. "That muthafucker is filthy! That is so messed up, but Stephen knows how touchy of a topic your relationship with your mother has always been for you. Maybe, Stephen is lying. Do you think he only said that to upset you? Do you really think Sandra would do something that lowdown?" Lorraine asked.

"That lady has hated me my whole entire life, so her doing something so low would not at all be shocking. Maybe Stephen is telling the truth, maybe my toxic, hateful ass, mother did fuck him to be spiteful. It has been this way for so long, I don't understand what I ever did so wrong to her. She already never cared about the shit I been through, but to go this low and do this, is mind boggling. I should have known something was up. Not once has she ever come to the apartment to see Kyle nor has she ever extended the offer to help me get adjusted to being a new mom. Never felt like I had a mother to depend on. I always wanted the type of relationship with her that you have with Pat, but it has never been possible. My mother always rejected having any kind of bond with me" I said in between sobs.

"Calm down, Sheeda. That is okay because you still are doing a great job with Kyle. You are so attentive and dedicated. Look at how hard you have worked. You're such a strong person Sheeda. You worked two jobs and went to school at the same damn time. Give yourself some credit, girl. You are a great mother and you and Kyle will have the bond that you have always wanted to have with Sandra," Lorraine said.

"Thank you, Lorraine. I will show my son all the love I never got and will never trust his father with him, ever again! He gave my son beer, what the fuck! Oh God, please help me keep calm. I cannot get over what Stephen did. You know he also told me he has four sons down in North Carolina! I never knew anything about him having kids! Do you think I would have had a baby with him had I known he has four that he doesn't do shit for? I literally do not know this man at all. He resents Kyle and said that I ruined his life for "pinning" a baby

180

on him. He told me that I was fat since I had the baby and that he was turned off by me. He admitted to cheating with other girls, too, not just with my mother" I cried.

"Stephen has lost his entire mind! It hurts right now but one day you will thank him for revealing his true self, Rasheedah. At the end of the day, Stephen needed you, not the other way around. You and Kyle deserve so much better than what he can offer you guys. I have always stayed out of your relationship concerning him but I have to speak on it now because Kyle doesn't deserve to be exposed to this craziness. Maybe if he gets off of drugs and stops drinking, he can be a better man for you guys but until then, you need to depart from him," she said.

I shook my head in disagreement, "Lorraine he fucked my mother and bragged about it. It hurts to even speak the words! That is the lowest of the fucking low! How could anyone do something like that," I said still in disbelief.

"Sheeda, I cannot even imagine what I would've done if a muthafucker told me he was fucking my mother! That is so disturbing and hard to even imagine," Lorraine said shaking her head. "He takes grimy to a whole other level, they both do."

"It's not only that though, Lorraine. He beat my ass like I meant nothing to him as our son screamed wildly. He cheated on me. He called me black, ugly, and fat. I am done with his ass for good this time. I need you to look after Kyle because I know he called the police and they are looking for me for what I have done," I confessed lowering my head. "Honestly, I don't have any regrets. He was high out of his mind and was going crazy. I had no choice but to defend myself and my baby," I spoke calmly wiping my eyes.

"Sheeda you did what you had to do, and what any mother would do to protect herself and her baby. And of course, I will look after my godson, you already know," she said reassuringly.

"Thanks, girl. Do you have any clothes that I can wear? I need to get these bloody clothes off me, and I need a shower," I said.

"Of course, I do Sheeda. Let me get you squared away," Lorraine smiled.

*

A few days later I walked into the police station with my attorney and turned myself in. Upon surrendering to the police, I was arraigned and was officially charged with one count of assault with a deadly weapon and endangering the welfare of a child. I pled not guilty citing self-defense and posted bail. The case had taken time to progress through the court system, but I eventually got my day in court. It happened a day before my graduation from college.

My attorney presented a solid argument that I grabbed the meat cleaver in self-defense, fearful of being killed by

Stephen who was on a cocaine-induced path of rage. I was attacked during his rampage after the confrontation of Stephen giving our six-month-old son beer. Previous incidents of domestic violence were also presented before the court. The presiding judge accepted the testimonies of the responding officers, two of whom had responded to several previous domestic violence calls at our home, as evidence. Each of their accounts coincided with my claims of Stephen's extensive drug and alcohol abuse and as a result, his ongoing occurrences of violent behavior.

In the end, both charges were dismissed against me and later expunged from my record. The next day, I graduated from Seton Hall University with a Bachelor of Arts degree in Sociology. Ever since then my life has undergone a rebirth of sorts.

F.E.A.R. YOUR SANITY

Baby Daddy Blues

Deadbeat sperm donor, yes I am talking to you, you have no clue of what it is to be responsible.

This poem is for you baby daddy because rather than cuss you out I will be a lady

Never worth me stepping out of character to blast you and match your level of shady

Rather than spit in your face and harbor regrets, I will give you what you've never had, self-respect

Mother to your baby, in the beginning I was naïve and too overjoyed to have your baby son. That is until finding out that while it was my first time your trifling ass squirt into pussies for fun

A first for me, for you my son was not your only one. You walked this road four other times before, how could you

This is my baby daddy blues to you because sperm donor you have no clue. I have your son and suddenly you flip, all at once I become your enemy

Called me stupid bitch, a slut, a hoe but before making our baby you claimed to love me. Before baby boy, it was all peaches and cream, a beautiful lie, you sold me a drunken dream. All of these compliments, said I was your Queen

Your coco goddess, your so-called everything. But once baby boy arrives, we are no longer Bonnie & Clyde. Just Bonnie and Baby, all that you took, all that I willingly gave. And this is how you repay This is my baby daddy blues, your trifling ass has no clue

Our prince arrives and the real you surface
Frequenting titty bars dropping money on coke and hoes
no concerns about the rent being due
I did this to myself, I am just as irresponsible
This is my baby daddy blues and your user ass has no clue
Constantly whining, bitching and complaining about all that you do
I pay this, I work long hours, I did this, I did that for you
Dude you created a family, providing is what you were supposed to

do. Hold shit down like a real man, while our seed was not planned
being the head of the household comes with being a man, something
you clearly do not understand

The more I expected, the more you pulled away, we would fight hard
I left so many times, baby does not deserve to be scarred
all because grown ass people made grown ass decisions and can't
get it right

I choose love, my Prince is now the only priority in my life
Living apart alone with our son was never my plan
But as long as I have breath in my body, I will do the very best
that I can for my little man

Encouragement, consistency, lot of memories we will share
I had my son very young, no regrets, but I have a message for the
youth out there

To all the young girls this one's for you, don't settle for a baby
daddy, a husband awaits you

Never sell yourself short, settling for a man with empty pockets and
promises. Manipulative ways, that ain't the one for you, something
real will be tried and will be true

Don't make lifelong commitments with temporary relationships, I am
speaking from experience. Love takes time and is not short term, took
some years but was a hard lesson to learn

Labor Day Spectacle

I arrived at the park over an hour late for my mother and stepdad's annual Labor Day cookout. For the past fifteen years, Mother and Otis have held the celebration in South Mountain Reservation, a well-kept nature reserve along the beautiful Rahway River with over two thousand acres of rolling hills. Each year the crowd seemed to double in size and this year was no exception. There were at least three hundred family, friends, and associates gathered to enjoy the holiday weekend.

My husband Warren, and son, Kyle and I unloaded our lawn chairs and walked towards the large group of familiar faces. I began dating Warren shortly after I ended my relationship with Kyle's father, Stephen. Warren and Kyle have a great father-son relationship that reminds me of the admiration of my own stepdad, Otis.

At thirty-one years old I still looked forward to the fried fish that Otis made to order at every barbeque he and mother hosted. So, just as soon as I could find a spot to sit my lawn chair down, I walked to join other partygoers in line as they waited their turns to get some hot fried whiting fish.

"Hello Rasheedah," I heard a familiar voice ask from behind me. The plate that I held in my hands dropped as my hands began to tremble. I could not believe what I had just heard, I must be hallucinating again, I thought to myself. Wake up, Rasheedah! Snap out of it girl, you are having another bad dream.

"I said, hello Rasheedah, how are you, how's life?" I heard the voice again. I stood still hoping that I would snap out of my dream but then the voice grew closer and louder over the music, "how have you been?" the man touched my elbow.

Realizing that this was no dream, I flinched, "get your fucking hands off of me!" I reacted as I turned around to face Timothy. He stood motionless at my reaction. Despite my aggression, only a few of the guests standing nearby noticed. The park was crowded and the music was loud, so I felt compelled to release what I had kept bottled up inside of me for many years. I could not believe he was standing before me. "Don't you ever in your fucking life put your hands on me! Those days are over, you twisted pervert! I am not a child anymore, nor am I your little plaything. The days of you and your filthy brother hurting me and, taking advantage of me are over you sick son of a bitch!" I yelled.

"Rasheedah, I was only saying hello. Not sure what you are talking about. I am a married man of God and I do not want any problems," he turned to walk away. His comment came across as bold and arrogant and I could not control my rage.

"You know exactly what the fuck I am talking about! Don't even try to play the dumb role! You weren't a man of God when you stole my virginity and fucked me in my asshole, you sick muthafucker!" I screamed drawing attention to myself. As a crowd began to gather around Timothy and me as I continued to unleash on him, "you are a rapist and scum of the fucking earth! How dare you even show up here? Who invited you!?" I exclaimed.

"I did! I invited him to my party, and you need to stop making an ass of yourself! What the hell is going on here? Whatever it is, now is not the time!" Mother warned as she began to break up the crowd that had gathered. "Nothing to see here people, everything is fine. Continue to enjoy yourself. Don't pay this wacko no mind," Mother spoke callously cutting her eyes at me. "You need to cut it the fuck out, you're embarrassing me," she mumbled softly so that I was the only one who could hear her.

"Sandra, I don't want any problems. I don't know what I did to Rasheedah, but had I known things would get out of hand in this way, I never would have accepted your invite. I have my wife and children over there, this is not what we came here for," Timothy spoke sorrowfully to mother who was staring at me with fury. "Me and my family are going to go, but thank you for the invite," he shook his head with humiliation.

"No, Tim! You are not going anywhere I will not have of it! Rasheedah is the one with the problem, so if anybody's going anywhere, it will be her ass!" Mother said looking at me.

"Everywhere you go you cause problems. You have been that way since you were a kid. A complete thorn in my ass! If you have a problem, then you need to go. Tim and his lovely family are welcome here just like everyone else I invited. This is my party, you do not have to be here," she said walking away and smiling apologetically to some of the guests who witnessed the commotion.

My husband, Warren, ran over to see what the disturbance was all about, "Rasheeda, what's wrong?" he asked looking at Mother. "What's going on here?"

"Warren, get your wife before I hurt her feelings," Mother said walking past me and bumping me on my shoulder. "She is always ruining everything. Always creating chaos everyplace, she goes. You are crazy to have married that psycho bitch," she said.

"What kind of mother invites her daughter's rapist to a cookout!? A psycho mother that does not care! A sorry excuse of a mother, that's who!" I shouted causing the onlookers to gather again for the spectacle that was about to stir again.

I stood firm prepared for the altercation as some of the attendees stared at me with shame, disappointment, curiosity, and even humor. To them, I had created a scene that had disturbed the peaceful environment of the barbeque. To me, I was finally confronting my oppressor, the man who had stolen my innocence, the one who had violated and brutalized me. The man who haunted me even as a thirty-one-year-old married woman with her own child. I felt zero shame but rage. In that moment, I wanted my mother to hurt like I was hurting.

"Listen to this everybody, what kind of mother would do such a thing to her own daughter? You all heard her. I am a crazed wacko for being devastated that she invited the man who raped me to her bourgeoise shindig," I yelled letting out a loud phony outburst of laughter.

"You selfish little bitch, how dare you to come to my gathering and make a scene! You need to go, right now! Warren, I am sorry but y'all gotta go. Blame your bitch of a wife! Holding on to shit that happened over twenty years ago that I am not so sure was forced onto her! What a psycho! She needs to put on her big girl panties and grow the fuck up!" she exclaimed with rage. "You have embarrassed me for the last time, get the fuck out of here!" she continued.

Otis walked over to Mother, "Sandra, what is going on here? Calm down, why are you hollering like that?" he asked.

"Ask Rasheedah's dumb ass! I am so sick and tired of her always causing problems. She is miserable and wants to make everyone else miserable," she spat. "Enough is enough! Pack your shit up and leave right now!" Mother shouted.

"Okay, mother-in-law," Warren said.

"Honey don't even worry about it. I will go get Kyle so that we can get out of here," my husband spoke softly. "Apologies for the commotion Otis, I don't even know what happened," Warren said to my stepdad.

"Warren, I wish these two would try to get along for one day. I want you and Rasheeda to come over tomorrow morning so that we can discuss this. Enough is enough, we are family and need to get to the bottom of this," Otis said disappointedly.

"What happened is your wife is an evil bitch who cannot let go of the past! She wants to play the victim for something she enjoyed until she got caught," Mother said.

"Well, now mother-in-law I am going to have to disagree with you. I have been married to Rasheeda for many years now and I know that whatever she endured has dramatically impacted her life so much so that it as well has impacted my and Kyle's lives. Even when we first met while working for the State of New Jersey and began dating, I immediately recognized how intense her anxiety issues were," Warren said before I interjected.

"Have you lost your mind? You stupid bitch, that man raped me multiple times and so did his brother! I was a child! How stupid do you sound telling me that I enjoyed a grown man sticking his dick in my ass and pussy until it bled! You are a horrible and such a poor excuse for a mother. I hate your guts!" I screamed. Otis held me in his arms as I sobbed watching my mother as she walked away.

"Calm down, gal. Don't get yourself all worked up," he said.

"I cannot believe this is how she is. Why would I make up something like that? She really believes I enjoyed them hurting me for years," I cried.

"Rasheedah, calm down," Otis continued to rub my back. "Of all days, why would this subject come up today?" he asked.

"She invited Miles's brother and his family here. Timothy, the man who raped me is at this cookout," I said.

"What? Where is he at?" Otis asked. I pointed to Timothy, who was a couple of yards away sitting on a blanket with his wife and two small children. Mother had reassured him that he was welcome and so he sat with his family enjoying the day as if he did not have a care in the world. Otis began walking over to Timothy who stood up when he recognized him approaching nearer to him and his family.

"Hey, what's going on Mr. Otis?" Timothy asked respectfully.

"Hello, I'd like to have a word with you over here," Otis spoke calmly as he and Timothy walked a few feet away from Timothy's family. "Listen, I do not know the specifics of what transpired between you and my daughter, but I cannot have you here. Whatever you did still has her extremely upset, which means I am extremely upset. I will not allow you here to further hurt her and disturb what is usually, for the past umpteen years, a peaceful family environment. So out of respect for her and me, I need you and your family to leave right now," Otis said.

"I will respect your wishes Mr. Otis," Timothy said. He returned to the blanket, packed up his belongings, and left the barbeque with his family.

Crumble

"Hey, good morning! Warren, Rasheedah, so good to see you, kids. How are y'all doing this morning," Otis asked jubilantly as we entered the kitchen. Otis was often admired by family and friends for his southern cuisine and today was no exception. The dining room table had already been prepared with a full selection of brunch items. The menu included Belgian waffles, sausage with peppers, fried apples, potatoes and onions, smothered chicken, bacon, eggs, homemade biscuits, strawberry preserves, and a variety of fruit juices. The table was beautifully decorated and welcoming.

"Everything looks so beautiful, Otis. Thank you for setting this up and preparing all of this food," Warren said.

"Not a problem at all," he said as he walked towards the stairwell, "Sandra! Come on downstairs when you get a chance, Warren and Rasheedah are here," Otis said.

Mother gracefully walked downstairs with a look of annoyance written all over her face.

"Good morning, mother-in-law," Warren greeted my mother with a smile and warm embrace.

"Morning Warren, how are you? Hello, Rasheedah," she said.

"Hello. So, Otis, what is the special occasion for all of this food you have prepared?" I asked.

"There is no particular special occasion, I figured we could all sit down together and enjoy some breakfast. I also think it would be a good time to resolve whatever caused the blowup at the cookout yesterday. Over the years I have witnessed the ongoing division between you and Sandra get worse and worse. It should not be this way, we are all family, you two are not strangers. You two are not each other's enemies, you are mother and daughter. How can we get to a place where we all can respect one another and coexist?" Otis asked.

"Well, that selfish heifer made a goddamn fool of us both yesterday in front of hundreds of guests," Sandra shouted.

"Hold it, Sandra. Please stop with the name-calling. Don't you think we could get a lot more accomplished if we tried listening to one another," Otis reasoned.

"Respectfully, I completely agree with you Otis. Rasheedah was unaware that we would be discussing this. I feel like had she'd known, she never would have come here out of expectation that there would be more confrontation. I decided to come here this morning because what happened yesterday was so embarrassing and devastating for the entire family. Seeing my wife crumble after being approached by, who I now know to be the animal who raped her most of her childhood infuriates me. At that moment, I maintained my composure to avoid making an already bad situation worst. However, Rasheedah is my wife and Kyle is my son. They are my responsibility. I cannot allow anyone to intentionally disturb their peace. So, there has to be an explanation as to why this man was even there at a family gathering, to begin with. It is my hope that this is all one big mishap," Warren said optimistically.

"Sandra, would you like to explain why Timothy was even there?" Otis asked.

"He was there because I invited him and his family just as I invited hundreds of other people who Rasheedah disrespected by creating a spectacle. Look Warren, Rasheedah may be your boss, but I be damned if she thinks she will be the boss of me! She is always making everything about her. I be goddamn if she will dominate an event that I have been hosting for all of these years," Sandra exclaimed.

"Warren, I am not doing this today. I am ready to leave," I stood up from the dining room chair.

"Honey, if this exchange will only be a continuation of what occurred yesterday, then I am on board with you and we should leave," Warren replied as he too stood up from the table.

"Don't let the door hit ya, where the good Lord split ya," Sandra exclaimed.

"Sandra, would you please stop this!" Otis exclaimed. "You don't have to be so rude, and nasty."

"Yes, she does Otis because it is who she is. Why can't you see that after all of these years?" I asked.

"Rasheedah, you are just like her at times. You both tune each other out and shut the other one down. I invited us all to come together to put all the cards on the table. Can you please sit down and sort this out? I am asking you to do this one favor for me, please," Otis pleaded.

Warren and I sat down in unison. I closed my eyes and silently prayed for God to guide my words.

"Otis, yesterday was a nightmare that came true. After all the years that have gone by of not seeing anyone from Miles's family, the one person who shows up is the one who forced me to perform sexual acts repeatedly on him and his brother. Can you understand why I was distraught at the sight of him? He attacked me for years. He made me feel less than dirt. He shattered my innocence. He reinforced his violent behavior by calling me every horrible name you could think of. And he laughed about it. And so did his brother Randy. All under the roof of Miles's family home. Where was my protection? Who was there to defend me against these grown ass men?" I asked as I began to sob.

Warren brought his chair closer to me and held my hands in his.

"Oh, my love, I am so sorry you had to endure that. Come here, honey," Warren held back tears as he held me in his arms.

"Oh my God," Mother huffed and rolled her eyes.

"I went through hell. I went through hell for years on account of her abandoning me and my brothers by going into the army and leaving us behind as if we didn't mean anything. As if we were not her responsibility. I have my own child now and cannot ever imagine abruptly skipping out on my commitment to be his mom. By the time I got to his age right now, I had been brutally assaulted and molested by multiple people. Where was she to protect me, to save me?" I screamed.

"Rasheedah, I know, I know it hurts. Try to calm yourself, you don't want to get yourself all worked up and have to go to the hospital," Otis said.

"Otis, this may be too much," Warren said flatly.

"I am done with the dramatics!" Sandra stood up and walked out of the dining room.

"Run, run run! That is what you have been good at my entire fucking life!" I shouted behind her.

"Sandra, please come back here. Rasheedah is your daughter and here she is crumbling before your very eyes. She is telling you, she is crying out to you and yet again you choose again to walk away?" Warren yelled.

"Sandra, you need to come back here, now," Otis spoke sternly.

"She does not care! She never has cared what those men did to me. If she cared she never would have anything to do with them. She would have pressed charges, but she did not.

Instead, she is friendly with the men who did this. Not to mention the allegations that Stephen says went on," I said.

"Rasheedah, shut the hell up! Stephen is lying, so don't you dare even go there! That is not what happened. As for Timothy and Randy, I was not there so I cannot say what all went on! I went into the army to provide for you and your brothers. I did what I felt was right at the time and you will not keep holding me hostage for the decisions that I felt was best at that time," mother screamed.

"Sandra, she was a child so how can you make a statement saying that you don't know what went on? That bastard is way older than Rasheedah which means he was grown when she was a child. I wish I'd known all that transpired, I would have shot that muthafucker dead as a doornail. And what did Stephen say," Otis hollered.

"A bunch of bullshit that ain't worth talking about! Oh please, Rasheedah is only telling you her version of what happened. Unbeknownst to her, Rodney and Rahmel both told me that on more than one occasion miss grown-ass would run away to go do the nasty with little boys in the neighborhood! She was nowhere to be found and even one time the police had to go out and find her. They found her hours later and brought her fresh hot-in-the-pants ass home!" she exclaimed.

"You fucking bitch, I hate you! I hate you! You have no idea what the fuck you are talking about! I ran away because I got tired of being raped!" I screamed at the top of my lungs.

"Yeah, yeah, yeah, cry me a fucking river!" Sandra shouted and went upstairs.

The Delivery Is in the Details

After my morning taping of The Sunday Show, I jumped on the Capital Beltway towards the south of downtown D.C. for my 11am therapy appointment with Isaiah. I was listening to the Heart and Soul channel of Sirius XM Radio when a familiar song began to play, Something in My Heart. I had not heard that song in many years. Whenever it would typically come on, I would change the channel because it always brought me back to a dark place of devastation but today was different. For the first time in over thirty-plus years, the song was enjoyable to listen to. I listened to Michel'le harmonize the lyrics and even sang along.

I pulled into the office parking lot to Isaiah's office feeling like I had conquered a marathon. A song that once symbolized pain no longer triggered me. Proud of myself, I hopped out of the truck and walked into Isaiah's office. The emphasis of walking instead of running when I felt that the coast was clear revealed the utmost sign of progress. Over the past several months of going to therapy on a continual basis, I began to notice small changes in myself but today was when I recognized how much of a considerable change my life had undertaken after nearly a year of working through my issues with Isaiah.

My anxiety was becoming less significant, and I even eliminated having panic attacks altogether when the doorbell randomly rings. Another major hurdle happened when my husband gave me a surprise fortieth birthday party with a group of our closest friends. For as long as I could remember I never liked surprises due to my worries of a poor turnout, something going wrong, or just being around a large crowd. However, my fortieth celebration was something special and I appreciated my husband's efforts. There was a stark difference in my reaction from previous times when he had tried to surprise me. This time I was warm, welcoming, and receptive to my guests and I did not freak out at any point. Since the start of therapy, my overall demeanor went from high anxiousness, uneasiness, and over-alert to a more relaxed, calmer, and unassuming mindset. I was beginning to feel more and more comfortable with myself just as I am, with no filter, no desire to please, or even to overaccommodate anyone. The positive progress of having gone to therapy was improving my overall quality of life so much that I was committed to my healing more than I'd ever been.

"Isaiah, I was able to listen to Michel'le sing Something In My Heart without breaking down or turning off the radio! I literally listened to the entire song on the way over here and even sang along with her! Can you believe that?" I exclaimed with excitement.

"I absolutely can believe that! Congratulations, on such a major achievement. I feel like you are on the right path to turn all of the trauma into triumph," Isaiah said.

"Never in a million years could I have imagined listening to that song which once signified so much hurt and pain. When I was listening to it, I didn't even recognize what it once symbolized. I am crying yes, but these are tears of joy," I exclaimed wiping my face.

"Rasheedah, you are doing exactly what you are here to do, and that is to face everything and recover your sanity!" Isaiah exclaimed as he handed me the box of Kleenex tissues.

"I am doing something I never thought possible. Letting go of the hurt that I have harbored for many years," I admitted.

"Imagine how expensive carrying that load has cost you over the span of forty years. Imagine how much holding on to the burdens of hurt, disappointment, and shame has hindered you from reaching your highest potential. You are healing girl. I can see the change in your eyes, your smile, and your heart. Take a bow," he said as he began to clap for me.

"Thank you, thank you, you are far too kind," I smiled as I took a bow.

"If your mother was sitting in this office with us, what do you think she would say?" Isaiah asked.

"She probably would not say much, maybe she'd pretend to celebrate and join you in applauding, but it would only be to save face and to appease you.

"Rasheedah, let's give her the benefit-of-the-doubt in this instance. In doing so, let's pretend that she also was not damaged from her own childhood trauma, abusive relationships, and abandonment issues. If we eliminate those preexisting factors that occurred before you were born, do you think your mother would show you compassion or still show herself as unavailable to your need for emotional support and reassurance?" Isaiah asked.

"She is disingenuous, Isaiah. She does not love me, she never did," I replied flatly.

"What if I told you that your mother's under-parenting and disconnection from you as her only daughter may directly correlate to her abandonment issues and lack of relevance in her own mother's life?" he asked.

I remained silent.

"What if beneath the surface there is generational trauma that goes even deeper than feeling rejection from your mother? We know that your maternal grandmother, Betty Lynn, abandoned your mother, your aunt, and your uncle. What if your grandmother, Betty Lynn, endured a similar strained connection with her mother, which would be your maternal great-grandmother?" he continued.

I remained silent.

"In the year that I have counseled you, it is apparent to me there are generational patterns shaping the overall picture. These patterns need to be explored because such an assessment can help us to identify life events that shifted how family members relate to each other. The two generational patterns that I see stem from abandonment and rejection. You had an emotional hunger to connect with your mother on a level where you two could have a strong mother-daughter bond. The issue is this, Rasheedah. I don't think your mother has the tools to offer you the closeness you have been starved of. Her mother was absent from her life and so, where would she have gotten the tools?" he asked.

I remained silent as the tears welled up.

"I could be wrong, maybe, maybe not but could it be possible that your mother resented you for exposing her shortcomings, which are vulnerabilities that she never FEARED – faced everything and recovered for the benefit of her sanity?" Isaiah asked.

"My mother hates me and never even cared that I was raped multiple times because of her negligent parenting," I cried.

"There is a major lack of acknowledgment of the trauma you have experienced. I don't know why your mother would be as harsh as it appears other than guilt and envy. Guilt because at some level her absence caused significant harm. Envy, because despite the harm, you still managed to persevere and climb the hurdles that she may have not been able to defeat as it relates to her own traumatic experiences," he said.

"Wow," I said and remained quiet.

"In a perfect world, what could she have done? What would supporting you through this look like in a perfect world," he asked.

"Well," I said.

"Actually, let's do this. I will give you a homework assignment because we need to wrap up today's session. I want you to go home and write your mother a letter explaining why you feel the way that you feel. Don't skim over or make general statements, be as precise and granular as possible when expressing what has caused the breakdown in the relationship with your mother," he said as I got up to leave.

"Okay, I will write the letter tonight," I said leaving Isaiah's office and heading home.

F.E.A.R. YOUR SANITY

A Letter to You

All that I ever wanted was your presence, guidance, and unconditional love. It really is not complicated, and it never has been. Yet, somehow, I always fell short in receiving the same affection, compassion, and attention that was shown to my brothers. Being the only girl, I never expected special attention but did have an expectation to equally feel maternal love and accessibility. The truth is that my siblings and I are different, and each held in a different regard than the other. It is apparent in how you engage with us, how you show support, how you communicate, how you parent, how you relate. I never wanted to be recognized as the black sheep of the bunch either but that is what my experience has been for as long as I can recall. To this day, I still do not understand why the mother-daughter relationship that I always yearned for was never within our grasps. We always seemed to clash and the more I fought for a place in your heart, the more and more I sought for the maternal support that all children yearn for, the more you always seemed to withdraw away from me. It was like I was the runt of the litter, and you went out of your way to limit your availability to me.

Our strained relationship still impacts me today, even as an adult. The side effects have been long-lasting and manifest in different ways. One way it impacts me is that it fractured my self-confidence from early on. I honestly never felt like you loved me or even liked me. While I appreciate the things that you have done for me it always felt like they were done out of obligation as opposed to love. Prior to the rapes and sexual molestation, I cannot recall a time when you ever hugged me or even told me that you loved me. That has profoundly impacted my life. I sought validation and love in all of the wrong places, and in all of the wrong people. I am thankful that I was somehow able to recover from the irresponsible paths taken in my younger years that could have easily ruined my life, all because I longed for love and acceptance.

This letter is not to bash you or to use your words "hold you hostage to the mistakes you have made in the past." This letter is to release you from any preconceived notions of what a mother-daughter relationship should look like or what I hoped it to be. All of the rage and disrespect that I bestowed as a result of feeling like you let me down was unacceptable. I had no right and apologize for my misconduct. I wanted you to be what I envisioned and perhaps this is where the disconnect started to begin. I wanted you to be something that you could not.

Above all, I wanted to be heard and acknowledged. For many years, I was captive to sexual violence. I hated you for not being there when I needed you but I hated you even more for refusing to hear me when you did return. You tuned me out whenever I tried to inform you of my experiences. I needed you to acknowledge my pain. I needed you to care. I needed you to get me the help that I needed to live, and not perish. I needed you to advocate for me and hold the offenders accountable. I needed you to show up for me. It felt like you did not even seem to care. Your doubt broke my heart and hurt me deeply. It still does. Even now there are times when I still feel voiceless and powerless.

To add to that, you never tried to dispel what Stephen alleged. His insinuation and your disinterest to cast away any doubt in my mind have confirmed that something did happen between you and him. I could never wish this type of pain on even my worst enemy. If you did do what Stephen alleges, your betrayal speaks more to your lack of self-respect than it could ever speak of your disrespect of me. It is low and gut-wrenching to think about so I will digress with confidence that God will work to avenge such disloyalty on my behalf.

To this day, as an adult, trust and loyalty have become paramount fixtures in my life. It takes me a while to tear down my walls of caution of others, but when it finally happens, I have a high expectation of maintaining that solid foundation because of the time it took to establish it. My tolerance of anyone disregarding my feelings is zero. If my feelings are not respected or held in the highest regard by those who claim to love me, then I do not need them. They are undeserving of a place in my life, and I can love these types from a distance.

Therapy has challenged me in ways I never imagined. Writing this letter to you has awakened all of life's possibilities. A weight is lifted, I feel lighter and no longer paralyzed by humiliation or shame about what I have overcome. That is right, I am an overcomer!

I release all the immense hurt, fear, and hatred of those who have hurt me. Forgiveness must start somewhere, and it begins and ends with me.

Mother, I forgive and release you. And in doing so, I feel so liberated.

Forgiveness is for you.

Free yourself and forgive them even if they truly are not sorry.